Dear Reader,

Their New-Found Family is a book very dear to my heart. When I was seventeen, I traveled to Europe on the Queen Elizabeth and experienced Hurricane Carrie, which made us two days late getting into port. I was on my way to boarding school in Lausanne, Switzerland, where I spent a glorious year learning French, meeting girls from all over the world and traveling through Europe on holidays. It's inevitable that some of my experiences would make their way into my books. In the case of *Their New-Found Family*, it was a trip down memory lane, one I hope you'll enjoy—especially because of the unique, special love between Rachel and Tris.

Rebecca Winters

Rebecca Winters, whose family of four children has now swelled to include three beautiful grandchildren, lives in Salt Lake City, Utah, in the land of the Rocky Mountains. With canyons and high Alpine meadows full of wildflowers, she never runs out of places to explore. In addition to her favorite vacation spots in Europe, they often end up as backgrounds for her Harlequin Romance® novels, because writing is her passion, along with her family and church.

Rebecca loves to hear from her readers. If you wish to e-mail her, please visit her Web site at www.rebeccawinters-author.com

THEIR NEW-FOUND FAMILY

Rebecca Winters

HARLEQUIN®

TORONTO • NEW YORK • LONDON
AMSTERDAM • PARIS • SYDNEY • HAMBURG
STOCKHOLM • ATHENS • TOKYO • MILAN • MADRID
PRAGUE • WARSAW • BUDAPEST • AUCKLAND

ISBN 0-373-18213-9

THEIR NEW-FOUND FAMILY

First North American Publication 2005.

Copyright © 2005 by Rebecca Winters.

All rights reserved. Except for use in any review, the reproduction or utilization of this work in whole or in part in any form by any electronic, mechanical or other means, now known or hereafter invented, including xerography, photocopying and recording, or in any information storage or retrieval system, is forbidden without the written permission of the publisher, Harlequin Enterprises Limited, 225 Duncan Mill Road, Don Mills, Ontario, Canada M3B 3K9.

All characters in this book have no existence outside the imagination of the author and have no relation whatsoever to anyone bearing the same name or names. They are not even distantly inspired by any individual known or unknown to the author, and all incidents are pure invention.

This edition published by arrangement with Harlequin Books S.A.

® and TM are trademarks of the publisher. Trademarks indicated with ® are registered in the United States Patent and Trademark Office, the Canadian Trade Marks Office and in other countries.

www.eHarlequin.com

Printed in U.S.A.

CHAPTER ONE

"UNCLE TRIS? Grand-pere just called. He'll be out front in a minute to drive you to the train station."

"I'm almost ready. How about you? Is your bag packed?"

Alain nodded. "It's in the foyer. Wish I were going with you," he muttered.

Tris didn't like the situation, either. When his blond, twelve-year-old nephew was upset, his blue eyes grew soulful and he looked so much like Tris's deceased elder brother, Bernard, it twisted something painful inside Tris.

"I'll only be gone two weeks. You're going to have a great holiday with the grandparents at Lake Como," he said, trying to sound upbeat.

Alain didn't respond to the remark. His nephew had grown so morose this past week, it worried him.

"By the time I'm back, we'll still have half

the summer left to go camping and fishing. Enjoy this vacation. There'll be a lot of guys your age to hang around with. I've arranged for Luc's parents to let him join you for part of the time."

"I know."

Nothing Tris said made a difference. The two of them had been inseparable for the last year. Tris had hoped his nephew's initial depression was a thing of the past. But knowing his uncle would be away for two weeks had changed the climate. Tris feared this separation was going to undo a lot of the progress Alain had made.

Since Tris had taken over the guardianship of his nephew who'd lost his parents in a car accident a year ago, the love he'd always felt for Alain had caused him to slip into the fatherly role without realizing it.

After the funeral, Alain had gone home to live with Tris at his house in Caux, a small mountain village high above Lake Geneva. The grandparents lived below them in the town of Montreux, Switzerland, where the headquarters of their company, the Monbrisson Hotel Corporation was located.

This was the first time since the funeral they

would be apart for more than one night. Alain wasn't the only one feeling the wrench.

"I'm going to miss you, too, *mon gars*."

His nephew's face closed up. "Do you have to go?"

Tris hated to see him this fragile again.

"It's that, or jail."

"They wouldn't really arrest you, would they?"

"I'm afraid so. Not even a Monbrisson can escape. When you turn twenty, it's every Swiss man's duty. Remember, we don't have an army, we *are* an army."

"Do you hate it?"

"No. I'm looking forward to seeing a couple of my old friends from school."

"I think it's stupid. We're never in a war. What do you do while you're there?"

"We get to blow things up for fun."

He'd hoped his comment would produce a smile, but Alain was too sad to see the joy in anything. The boy looked up at him through cloudy eyes. "Do you want me to find your suitcase?"

"Actually I'm taking my backpack."

"I'll get it."

"Thanks. You'll find it in the big storage cupboard in the hall."

"Okay." Alain left the bedroom. When he came back, he was holding two packs.

Tris glanced at the old, dark green one in surprise. "I haven't seen that thing in years."

Alain tested the weight. "It's heavy."

While Tris started putting clothes in his military pack, he watched Alain out of the corner of his eye. His nephew began opening the pockets of the other pack.

"Hey—your hockey skates, and a puck! It's signed by Wayne Gretzky! I didn't know you'd met *him*."

"Neither did I," Tris murmured in surprise.

"There's a lot of junk in here." It was the first sound of excitement he'd heard in Alain's voice all week.

"You know what they say about one man's junk being another man's treasure."

"Can I keep it?"

The request didn't surprise Tris. His nephew was crazy about hockey though his parents had never allowed him to play it. "If you want it, it's yours."

"Thanks. Did you know you have a whole

slug of tags collected from the various cantons?"

"That's not surprising. I hauled everything around in that bag during my hockey years. For some reason I thought it had been tossed out a long time ago."

Alain dumped the rest of the contents in the middle of the bed. "You've got a bunch of American and Canadian money in here. How come?"

"According to your grandparents, before my hockey accident in Interlaken, I played an exhibition match with my team in Montreal, Canada.

"After it was over, the team members flew home. But for some reason I wanted the experience of traveling on a ship, so I went on the QE2. Since it sailed from New York, I must have spent a couple of days there.

"The ship landed in Southampton. From there I traveled to London and caught a flight back to Switzerland where I joined the team for training in Interlaken. At least that's what I've been told."

His nephew pored over the pile of stuff. "Here's an envelope with a picture of the QE2 on it. You don't remember anything about going on that ocean liner?"

"No. The concussion robbed me of those memories. All of them."

"I don't see how you could forget your trip."

"Neither do I, but it happened. The doctor told me the brain is like a giant blackboard. The blow to my head from the hockey stick erased some of the writing. The two weeks leading up to the accident, and the month after, are gone forever."

"That's so weird. Hey—did you know some girl left you a message in English on the inside of this envelope?"

He paused in the task of packing his T-shirts. "What does it say?"

In his best English Alain read, *"My love—I will never forget last night as long as I live."* He lifted his head. *"Oh la la*—Uncle Tris!"

Tris smiled, but deep inside he didn't like the sound of it. "Dare I ask if that's all she wrote?"

"Phone me ASAP," Alain continued to read. *"I'll meet you wherever you say, Tris darling."*
Tris?

His nephew flashed him a surprised glance. "I thought no one but our family had ever called you that."

Tris had to admit he was surprised, too. He'd been christened Yves-Gerard Tristan de Monbrisson. Except for family and one or two close friends, he was called Gerard. In professional circles no one would know him as Tris.

Tristan had been his mother's romantic contribution to his full name. It had been an embarrassment to him in his youth, so he'd always kept it a secret. Yet he'd revealed it to the stranger who'd penned the note.

His curiosity fully roused, he said, "I'm almost afraid to ask if there's more."

"There is!" Alain declared. *"You didn't have to make me promise to wear your ring around my neck. Don't you know there'll never be anyone else for me but you?"*

His ring? He'd never worn rings…except for one—a ring that had been presented to him by his hockey team.

That's where it had disappeared to?

"Our love is forever. Like you, I'll be counting the months until we're married. All my love, Rachel."

Tris stood there speechless.

He'd been involved with several women in the past whom he'd considered marrying. But in each case something elusive had always held him back from making a full commitment.

It was ludicrous to think that at nineteen, with only a year of university behind him, and a career in professional ice hockey in his future, he'd actually proposed to a girl. It didn't sound like him to be that impulsive or reckless. Not at all.

Yet the stranger's endearments, the mention of a ring and marriage—everything she'd said led him to believe theirs had been an intimate association, no matter how brief.

"What does ASAP mean?" Alain wanted to know.

"As soon as possible."

He squinted up at him. "You don't remember her even a little bit?"

A chill ran through him every time he was reminded of the period of his life which would always remain a total void. "Afraid not."

"She put her address at the bottom. *Le Pensionnat Grand-Chene, Geneve.*" Tris felt his nephew's gaze on him, eyeing him speculatively. "She must have felt awful when you never even called her."

That kind of observation coming from a twelve-year-old revealed how much more insightful Alain had become since losing his parents. But in this case Tris needed to apprise him of a few facts.

"I'm sure she forgot me as soon as she got off the ship. At that age, you think you're in love with every person you're attracted to."

Except that the mention of a ring he'd given her made a lie of what he was telling Alain. He wouldn't have parted with it unless—

"You mean you were just pretending that you wanted to marry her?"

He let out a frustrated groan. "Alain—I have no idea what actually transpired, or what we said to each other.

"Sometimes in the heat of the moment people read things into situations because they want them to be true. That was years ago. The fact is, at nineteen I lived for hockey, not girls."

"Maman and Papa fell in love when they were nineteen," his nephew persisted.

"They were the exception because their attraction turned into a lasting love. There's a big difference between that and hormones. You do know what they are?"

"Yes. Hormones get you in trouble, like having a baby before you're old enough to be a good father or mother."

"Exactly. Your parents taught you well. Don't ever forget it."

"Can I ask you another question?"

"Of course."

"Do you love Suzanne?"

"Did your grandmother ask you to ask me?"

"Yes."

Alain's honesty was one of the qualities Tris admired most in his nephew.

"I thought so."

"She says Suzanne's been your receptionist for a long time, and that one day you'll discover she's the one you've loved all along."

"Maybe your grandmother's right, but it hasn't happened yet."

"I'm glad," Alain said, looking relieved.

Tris was aware his nephew had a hard time sharing him with anyone else.

"Just so you know, I've always made it a policy not to date employees, Alain. Some day if you decide you want to come into the hotel business with me and your grandfather, you'll understand why it's necessary to separate our work from pleasure.

"When the right woman comes along, I'll know it and do something about it."

"Maybe this Rachel was the right one, and

that's why you've never been able to love any-one else, even though you don't remember her."

"That's something I'll never know. By now I'm sure she's married and has several children," Tris muttered, wanting to change the subject.

Alain's comment shouldn't have bothered him, but the fact remained that even though it had been twelve years, those six blank weeks of his life still haunted him.

He heard the horn honking, bringing him back to the present with a jolt. His housekeeper poked her head in the door.

"Do you wish me to tell your father to come in the house to wait?"

"*Non merci, Simone.* We'll be right down."

"*Tres bien.*"

One last pair of heavy tube socks stuffed into the top pocket of his military pack and he was ready.

"Sounds like your grandfather's getting im-patient. Let's go."

"Okay." Alain put everything back in the pack he'd adopted. The two of them left the bedroom and went down the stairs to the front hall. Alain grabbed his suitcase and went out the front door to put his things in the trunk. Tris followed.

"Enfin!" his father said when he joined them with his pack.

"Sorry to keep you waiting, Papa, but Alain and I had some man-to-man business to discuss."

His father's blue eyes twinkled as he looked at his grandson. "In that case, I understand." He shut the lid of the trunk and they all got in the car.

The senior Monbrisson revved the engine before negotiating the steep, winding road that led down to Montreux. In the distance, the shimmering waters of Lac Leman reflected a pale blue. It was a sight Tris loved and never grew tired of.

Too soon they arrived in front of the *gare*. Tris levered himself from the back seat, then retrieved his pack from the trunk. He leaned inside the passenger window to kiss his nephew. "I'll phone you every night to see how you're doing."

With tear-filled eyes, Alain caught him around the neck. The boy was suffering. Tris could relate.

One minute his brother and sister-in-law had been alive. In the next, they were gone. He still had a hard time believing it, so he could just imagine Alain's pain knowing he'd never see his parents again.

But Tris recognized that right now his nephew's greatest problem was the fear his uncle wouldn't come back again, either.

"When I return, we'll go camping. How's that?"

Alain simply nodded.

While they hugged, Tris's father sent him a silent message that said he would do everything possible to lift Alain's spirits.

Raising him had become a family affair, yet everyone was aware the boy clung to Tris.

He walked around the other side of the car and kissed his father on the cheek. "Call me if things get bad," he whispered.

After turning away, he strode swiftly toward the entrance to the train station. Besides his heart being torn having to leave his nephew, old demons had been resurrected by the note Alain had found in the backpack.

Over the years Tris had pretty well learned to control the panicky sensation of not being able to remember that period of his life.

But for no accountable reason, this new evidence of past events with a girl—apparently intimate events which had transpired without his having any knowledge of them—made him uneasy. He could feel one of those damn headaches coming on.

"Alain?"

"Oui, Grand-mere?"

"I'm going out in the garden to finish some weeding. I'd like to get it done before we leave for Lake Como in the morning. Do you want to help me?"

"I'll be down in a few minutes," he called to her from the top of the stairs.

"Tres bien."

The moment his grandmother's footsteps faded, he rushed into the bedroom which had been his father's growing up. He always stayed in there on overnight visits.

There was a phone on the bedside table. Alain hurried over to it and picked up the receiver to call Guy, his uncle's assistant, on his cell phone.

"Bon apres-midi, Alain. What can I do for you?"

"I need your help, but you can't tell Uncle Tris about it."

"It will be our secret as long as it's not illegal, immoral or dangerous."

"Guy—"

"I'm teasing you. Go on."

"Okay. I'm trying to help my uncle remember the memories he lost because of his accident. He worries about it sometimes."

"I know," Guy murmured. "I can't say I blame him. It must have been very frightening to wake up in a strange hospital, not recalling anything that happened, and be forced to accept it. I admire him very much for his courage."

"So do I. That's why I've called you. I found out the name of a person who'd been with him right before he got hit with that hockey stick."

"Tu blagues?"

"No, I'm not kidding." He filled Guy in on what he'd discovered in the backpack. "I'd like to talk to her, but I need you to get some information for me first."

"A shipboard romance, eh? This sounds intriguing. I'll do what I can."

"Good. Her name is Rachel Marsden." He spelled it for him. "I think she's Canadian or American. Anyway, she must have been a student. The address here says *Le Pensionnat du Grand-Chene, Geneve.* Do you think you could call the school and find out where she came from?"

"I'm afraid they won't give me that information without a good reason."

"You could tell them the truth, that you're trying to help Uncle Tris recover his memory."

"That just might work. You know something, Alain? You have your uncle's shrewd instincts. Hold on while I see what I can find out."

"Okay."

Alain sat on the side of the bed and waited. It seemed to take forever until Guy came on the line again. "The secretary said that the student in question was from Concord, New Hampshire, in the U.S.

"I called the information operator and was given her family's phone number. It's different from the one on her original application to the school. Do you have a pen?"

"Yes."

"I'm going to give you the country and city codes, too."

Alain wrote everything down. *"Merci, Guy!"*

"You're welcome. Let me know what you find out."

"I will."

He hung up, planning to call the number tonight. By that time it would be late afternoon on the East Coast. Hopefully Rachel Marsden's parents would be home.

Just as he reached the door to go downstairs and help his grandmother, the phone rang again. He dashed across the room to answer it, thinking it might be Guy calling because he forgot to tell him something.

"Hallo?"

"Alain?"

"Uncle Tris—" Guilt swept through him. "I thought you couldn't call me until tonight."

"I decided to surprise you and let you know I'd arrived safely."

"I'm glad."

"Are you all right?"

"Yes."

"What have you been doing so far?"

Alain's cheeks went hot. "On the way home from the train, Grand-pere took me to the boat show exhibit. What about you? How soon are you going to start blowing things up?"

His uncle laughed. Though Tris and his dad were completely different they sounded a lot the same over the phone.

"This week we're starting out with mountain climbing maneuvers. The good part won't come until the second half of training."

"I wish you didn't have to go anywhere."

"Well I'm here now, and before long it'll be over. How soon are you leaving for Lake Como?"

"*Grand-pere* said early in the morning."

"Have you found out when Luc's parents will be bringing him?"

"He called me a little while ago and said the day after tomorrow."

"Then you don't have such a big wait. That'll be fun to have your best friend with you."

"I guess. I hope you don't get a headache while you're gone."

"I haven't had one in several months."

His uncle was lying. "That's good."

"You know what? You worry too much, but I love you for it."

Alain's eyes smarted. "I love you, too. Please don't get hurt while you're climbing."

"I was just going to say the same thing to you. When you and Luc go out on the paddle boats, promise me you'll wear your life jackets. Sometimes the wind comes up unexpectedly. I had a close friend die on that lake in a summer storm because he wasn't wearing one."

"I promise."

"How are the grandparents?"

"Fine. I'm going outside in a minute to help them weed."

"I'm sure they'll appreciate your hard work and the company. I'll phone again tonight after they're back from their nightly walk and talk to all of you."

"Okay. *A bientot.*"

"Thanks for the ride, Mrs. Pearsoll." Natalie Marsden dragged her duffel bag from the trunk.

"You're welcome!"

"Phone me later, Nat," Kendra Pearsoll called from the window.

"I will."

Natalie ran up the walk to the porch of her grandparents' Georgian styled house and let herself in the front door with the key.

"Nana?" she called out. "I'm home." She hurried through the interior to the kitchen. Her grandmother had left a message on the fridge with one of the magnets Natalie had given her for her birthday.

She dropped her bag, then poured herself a glass of milk. While she drained it she read the note her grandmother left.

Natalie, I'm next door at Mrs. Bleylock's, look-ing at her newest little grandson. I guess your hockey practice took longer than usual. Come on over and see how cute he is. Love, Nana.

She grabbed an apple and started for the front door. If she didn't hurry, her mom would be by to pick her up before she could get a peek at the new baby.

She was halfway through the dining room when she heard the phone ring. It was probably her mom who'd left work and was letting her know she was on her way to pick her up. She retraced her steps to the kitchen and lifted the receiver.

"Hello?" she said, a trifle out of breath.

"Hello. Is this the Marsden residence?"

Whoever the boy was on the other end of the phone, he sounded foreign.

"Yes. Who's this?"

"My name is Alain. I'm looking for Rachel Marsden."

"That's my mom."

"Oh. Is she there?"

"No. Are you sure you have the right number?"

"Did your mother once go to school in Geneva, Switzerland?"

Natalie blinked. "Yes."

"Did she ever sail on the QE2?"

The mention of the ship gave Natalie butterflies on her insides. "Yes."

"Then she's the one."

Her hand absently fingered the end of her long, dark brown ponytail. "How do you know about my mom?"

"By accident I found out she was on the same ship as my uncle."

Natalie held her breath. "What was his name?"

"Tris Monbrisson."

Natalie tried to stop the gasp that came out of her mouth, but she was too late. Her eyes suddenly stung with tears. She felt like she was going to suffocate from pain...and excitement.

Wiping the moisture from her cheeks she said, "If your uncle wants to talk to her, why doesn't he call her himself?"

"*I'm* the one who wants to talk to her. He doesn't know I'm phoning."

Natalie's breath caught. "Why do you want to speak to her?"

"I need to tell her the reason why she never heard from him after they reached Switzerland."

Natalie's heart pounded so hard, she felt sick. "That was a long time ago. I don't think my mom would even remember him."

"If she married your father, then I guess my uncle was right."

"What do you mean?"

"He said she would have forgotten him the minute she got off the ship. I'll hang up now."

"No—wait!" she cried out. Dry mouthed she said, "What were you going to tell my mom? I want to hear."

"At my uncle's hockey camp, he got struck on the head by a hockey stick and went into a coma."

"A coma—"

"You know. Where you sleep and never wake up?"

"I know what it means." Fear shot through her. "I-is he okay now?"

"Yes. But when he woke up a month after his accident, he couldn't remember anything."

"You mean he had amnesia?"

"Yes. There are six weeks of his life wiped out of his mind. He never remembered playing hockey in Canada, or his trip back to Switzerland. Those memories are gone forever."

"You're kidding—"

"It's the truth. You can call the Belle-Vue Hospital in Lausanne. That's where bad head injury patients are taken. My uncle was there for a month!

"Ever since then he's been troubled because he doesn't remember anything about that time on the ship. Sometimes he worries so much, he gets bad headaches.

"I was thinking that if your mother called him to tell him about what happened while they were on board together, it would make him feel a lot better."

"How did you learn she was on the ship with him?"

"I was looking in an old backpack in his closet and found a note she wrote him on the ship's stationary. She put her address in Switzerland at the bottom. The school secretary said she came from New Hampshire. That's how I got this phone number."

"Oh my gosh— Listen Alain— Give me your number. I'll tell my mom you want to talk to her."

"Okay. Here are two numbers. Are you ready?"

"Yes." She'd reached for the pad and pencil her grandmother kept on the kitchen counter.

He gave her the information. While Natalie wrote down the digits, she could hear her mom honking out in front.

"I'll be at the second number for two weeks

starting tomorrow. Then I'll be back at this one."

"Okay."

"Tell her to call me at this exact same time."

"I will. Now I have to go. Goodbye, Alain."

"Goodbye."

She hung up and called her grandma at Bley-lock's to tell her she was going home with her mom. Then she hurried out to the car where her mom was waiting.

"Hi, honey!"

"Hi, Mom." Natalie leaned across the front seat to kiss her cheek.

"Before I left the office, Steve called," her mother said, reversing to the street. "He's taking us out to dinner tonight at the Brazilian Grill, so we're going to have to hurry to be ready on time. Friday nights mean a long line. If we're there early, there'll be time for a movie after."

"I don't want to go."

Her mother flashed her an anxious glance. "You look a little flushed. What's wrong, honey? Don't you feel well?"

"My stomach's kind of upset." It was the truth.

"Well I'm not leaving you if you're coming down with flu. It's going around." She reached out to touch her forehead with the back of her hand. "You feel warm. That settles it. I'll call Steve and cancel."

"Don't do that yet, Mom. I'm not sick the way you mean, but I do need to talk to you in private before we go anywhere."

In a few minutes they'd reached the house. She hurried inside. Her mom followed with the duffel bag Natalie had forgotten.

The concern in her parent's eyes had turned them a dark green, providing a contrast with her blond hair that made her more beautiful than any of her friends' moms.

When Natalie first met Steve, she'd heard him tell her mom how gorgeous she was. Even Kendra's dad had told Natalie, "Your mother's a real knockout."

Tris Monbrisson must have thought so, too. He'd asked her to marry him twelve years ago. But for that accident...

CHAPTER TWO

"WHAT'S wrong, honey?" Rachel Marsden put the bag on the floor.

"I have something to tell you. I think you'd better sit down."

At her daughter's tone of voice, a chill invaded Rachel's body. "Why? Does this have anything to do with your grandmother?"

Rachel's father had passed away two years ago. Her mother had taken it hard, but Rachel had thought she was doing a lot better these days. It would be unbearable to lose her mother, too. Rachel wanted her around for a long, long time.

"No—this doesn't have anything to do with Nana." After a slight hesitation she said, "Mom? While I was over there, someone called trying to find you."

Her brows knit together. "Who?"

"Alain Monbrisson."

Alain Monbrisson? Just hearing the name made Rachel feel faint. "That's what Tris called his baby nephew." She put a trembling hand to her throat. "I don't understand."

"Did you once write my father a letter on the ship's stationary?"

A moan escaped Rachel's lips. "Yes."

"Well, Alain found it in his uncle's old back-pack. He tracked you down through your school in Geneva and then phoned Nana's house. She was next door, so I answered it."

"Oh, no—"

"Don't worry, Mom. Alain doesn't know his uncle is my father. He thinks you're married and I'm another man's daughter."

"Honey—I didn't mean—"

"I know what you meant," Natalie broke in, sounding older than her eleven years. "The reason Alain was calling was to tell you about the terrible hockey accident that happened while my father was at hockey camp in Interlaken."

An accident—

"Sit down, Mom—you look like you're going to be sick."

Rachel felt sick. She sank down on the end of the couch. "Tell me what he said."

As she listened to her daughter, she started to tremble and couldn't stop.

Tris had been in a coma?

"Alain thinks that if you phoned his uncle and filled him in about your time together on the ship, it would ease his mind concerning the period of time he doesn't remember. Hopefully it will help cut down his headaches."

Tris could have died and Rachel would never have known. She buried her face in her hands.

"I was afraid to tell you about this because it changes a lot of things, Mom. I always thought my father was a horrible man to have hurt you the way he did. But now I know he didn't do it on purpose, I want him to know he has a daughter. Maybe he'll want to meet me. What do you think?"

What do I think?

With one phone call, the world Rachel had built so carefully for her and Natalie had just come crashing down around them.

She could hardly comprehend the fact that a block of amnesia was the reason Tris had vanished from her life.

If his nephew hadn't found that note, they would all still be in the dark. Unfortunately Natalie had been given enough information that it would take an act of nature to stop the rising tide of hope in her heart.

To be united with her father had always been

Natalie's dream, though she'd never expressed it verbally to Rachel.

Before Rachel did anything about the situation, she needed clarification on one certain point. It required talking to Alain Monbrisson herself.

She raised her head, smoothing the hair from her face. "Natalie, honey? Would you bring me Alain's phone number please?"

Her face glowed with excitement. "I'll be right back."

Rachel reached for her purse and pulled out her cell phone. When Natalie returned with the paper and pointed to the second number, Rachel started punching the digits.

She checked her watch. It was four in the States, making it around ten in Switzerland.

After three rings someone picked up. *"Hallo?"* said a young male voice.

"Hello. Is this Alain Monbrisson?"

"Yes?"

"My name is Rachel Marsden. I understand you were trying to find me."

"Hello, Ms. Marsden. Thank you for calling me back."

She couldn't fault his manners or his English.

"My daughter just told me of your conversation. I must admit hearing about your uncle's accident has come as a shock. We can all thank God he survived it."

"Yes. He could have died."

Rachel swallowed with difficulty. "Tell me something, Alain. Does he know you found the note I wrote him?"

The words she'd penned had poured straight from her heart.

"Yes. I read it to him while he was packing this morning."

She clutched the phone tighter. "But it was *your* idea to phone me, not his?"

"Yes."

His honesty came as an enormous relief. "Is he aware you phoned my parents' house in an effort to locate me?"

"No. He's gone away on a trip."

"I think you're a very special person to care about him. But much as I understand why you want to help your uncle, the need to talk to me has to come from him, not you.

"It's been twelve years. He's a thirty-one-year-old man now. If he were still that curious about his past, he would have followed up with a phone call to me.

"But he didn't because he's been on the road to recovery for a long time and believes it's better to leave things alone. I tend to agree with him.

"Some things in life *are* better left alone. So let this phone call between us be the end of it. Do you understand what I'm telling you?"

"Yes," came the quiet answer. "I won't tell him I talked to you or Natalie."

"Thank you. I'm sure if you think about it, you'll see it's the right thing to do. Are you familiar with the American expression, 'Let sleeping dogs lie'?"

"No."

"Well, it doesn't matter. The important thing is that he's alive and well today. I'm very happy for him and your family. Thank you for the call, Alain. Goodbye."

"Goodbye."

They both clicked off.

"How could you, Mother?" Natalie cried, white-faced.

Rachel steeled herself to stay in control. "I did what I had to do. Did Alain read you the note I wrote to your father?"

"No," she said, tight lipped.

"I'll tell you what it said." She gave her daughter the word by word account. "Even knowing what I'd written to him, your father didn't act on the information.

"He could have tried to contact me, just like his nephew did, if only out of curiosity. But he didn't. Instead—according to Alain—he went away on a trip not the least bit interested in following up."

Her daughter's face crumpled before she ran into her arms. Rachel absorbed the sobs that echoed in her own soul.

"I know this is so hard, honey." She kissed Natalie's hair and cheeks. "But we have to look ahead, not back. Don't you see? Your father's mind is a blank in regards to that period of his life. He's moved on, and probably has a wife and family.

"What's done is done. Too many years have gone by. That's how he honestly feels, otherwise he would have phoned us instead of his nephew making the call. What more proof do we need, huh?"

"I guess we don't," Natalie answered in a strangled voice. She finally pulled away and wiped her eyes.

"Come on. Let's get ourselves ready to go out to dinner."

Natalie hung back. "Mom? Do you like Steve?"

"Yes, but I haven't been going out with him very long."

"Do you think you could love him the way you once loved my father?"

"Honey, every relationship is different. Steve's growing on me."

"But it's not like it was when you first met my father."

She sucked in her breath. "No. Nothing will ever be like that again."

Natalie eyed her intently. "How come?"

"Because I was eighteen, impressionable and totally naïve about love. But I want you to know it was the best thing that ever happened, because I have you. You're my whole life! I love you so much you'll never know." She hugged her tightly again.

"I love you too, Mom."

"I know it's hard but let's forget this phone call ever happened."

"Okay."

"Hey—Tris—"

Tris was standing on the crowded *quai,* impatiently waiting for the train to pull into the station. At the sound of Claude's voice, he turned in his direction. His childhood buddy came running up to him.

"I've been looking all over for you since lunch. I just got off the phone with Giselle.

Why don't you come home with me this weekend? Her friend Helene is visiting from Neuchatel. She's a real babe."

He smiled. "If my nephew weren't waiting for me, there's nothing I'd like more." Since the funeral he'd been too preoccupied trying to help Alain cope to pursue an active social life.

His friend sobered. "How's he doing?" he asked as the train came into view.

"According to my parents, he's made it through these two weeks without falling apart."

"Sounds like progress."

"Of a sort. Thanks for the invite, Claude. Let's plan a ski trip in early December. By then I'm hoping Alain will be able to handle the separation better."

"I'll count on it." He patted his shoulder. *"Bonne chance."*

Tris nodded. "Give my best to your wife. Take care, *mon ami."*

Relieved to be getting back to Caux, Tris boarded the train and looked for a seat. When he couldn't find one he stood in front of the window at the entrance of the *voiture*, staring blindly at the passing landscape.

He had no doubts Giselle's girlfriend lived up to Claude's description of her. But even if it weren't for Alain needing him so desperately, he wouldn't have taken Claude up on his invitation.

Since hearing the words of the note Alain had found in the backpack, Tris had been haunted by them.

She must have felt awful when you never even called her.

Alain had said a mouthful. There hadn't been a moment in the last two weeks that Tris hadn't wondered about his relationship with Rachel Marsden.

He checked his watch. The train wouldn't reach Montreux for another hour. Time enough for him to call Geneva and make a few inquiries.

Perhaps the Pensionnat du Grand-Chene was still in business and could provide him with a little information about one of its former students. If the school no longer existed, he would have to let it go.

The operator found the number and within seconds he was put through to the *directrice*. When Madame Soulis came on the line he introduced himself.

"Monsieur Monbrisson! It's an honor to talk to you. I saw you on a recent television program about the expansion of your hotels in France. It was very impressive."

"Thank you, *madame*."

"How can I help you?"

"I'm inquiring about a student who attended your school twelve years ago."

"Twelve you say? Just a moment. I'll bring up that year on the computer."

"She was a friend of mine, but we lost track years ago and I don't have her old home address. Would it be possible for you to check your information for me?"

"*Bien sur.* What was her name?"

"Rachel Marsden."

"Rachel? *Ah, oui.* She was the lovely blond American girl who came to us in the fall. I remember her particularly because she became ill and returned to the States after only a few months."

The revelation sent an involuntary shudder through his body. Having to think fast he said, "That explains why I couldn't reach her."

"Yes. We were very sorry to see her go. She was an excellent student. Here is the number and address of her parents, Dr. and Mrs. Edward Marsden. As I recall, he was an eye surgeon."

Tris jotted down the information. "*Merci, madame.* You've been of immense help."

"*Pas de quoi, monsieur.*"

When they hung up, he immediately called

the international operator for New Hampshire to find out if Dr. Marsden still had the same phone number as before.

There'd been a change.

He wrote down the new number, telling the operator not to connect him. It was only seven in the morning on the East Coast. He'd give it another half hour, then call.

Before he clicked off, he asked the operator if a Rachel or an R. Marsden were listed. To his surprise there was a listing with an R. It could belong to either sex, of course. Nevertheless he took down the number before hanging up.

A certain percentage of married professional women used their maiden names for business purposes. In a few minutes he would check it out first before trying to reach her parents.

The train rounded a curve and passed through a tunnel. The darkness reminded him of that one portion of his life he couldn't remember.

Some friends from his old hockey team had long since filled him in on the time they'd spent together in Montreal. His family and doctors had been able to account for everything that had happened to him at his training camp and the subsequent accident that had put him in the hospital in Lausanne.

It was the time in between…the time on the ship and the period before he arrived at Interlaken that had eluded him all these years. In a while it was possible he would be able to talk to the woman who'd known him well enough to call him Tris.

When the train came back out into the sunlight, he should have felt a sense of relief that before the day was done, one phone call might give him closure on his past.

Yet a new dread had attacked him since learning Rachel Marsden had returned to the States a few months after arriving at the school because she wasn't well.

My love—I'll never forget last night as long as I live.

That one line from her note resounded in his head, causing him to break out in a cold sweat.

"Mom? Kendra's dad has come for us."

"Okay, honey. Have a great day. I'll pick you two up at the rink after hockey practice."

"Okay. Love you."

"I love you."

Rachel heard the front door close.

She finished brushing her hair, then slipped on her suit jacket, not wanting to be late for work. Rachel had fixed the girls' breakfast after their sleepover, not realizing how late it had gotten.

After a quick glance around the bedroom, she hurried downstairs to get her purse which she must have left in the kitchen. When the house phone rang, she assumed it was one of Natalie's friends who'd just missed her. She reached for the receiver.

"Hello?"

"Is this the Marsden residence?" The deep male voice on the other end spoke with only the slightest trace of accent, yet it sounded vaguely familiar.

She stirred uneasily. "Yes?"

"I'm looking for a Rachel Marsden. Do I have the right number?"

"W-who is this?" she cried softly.

After an extended silence, "Does the name Tris mean anything to you?"

Suddenly Rachel's legs grew weak. She started to tremble as memories came flooding back.

It *was* Tris.

People could age, but that was his voice, his fingerprint. Its unique timbre resonated in every particle of her body, overwhelming her. He was actually alive, speaking to her from the other end of the phone line.

"H-hello, Tris." Trying to control her panic she said, "I guess it was too much to expect that your nephew would be able to keep his promise."

There was another pause. "I'm afraid you have me at a disadvantage."

"Please don't pretend you didn't realize Alain already called me two weeks ago. H-he told me about your amnesia," she stammered, mortified by her loss of composure.

"I've been away on army maneuvers. Though I've phoned him every night, he never mentioned that he'd been in contact with you."

She drew in a shaky breath, trying to recover her equilibrium. "Are you saying you made the decision to call me all on your own?"

"Bien sur," he drawled with quiet irony. When he spoke in French, it was like she'd gone back in time where everything sounded so much more intimate.

"While I was preparing for my trip, Alain rummaged through an old backpack of mine and came across a note you'd written to me on board the QE2.

"I intended to track you down, but I couldn't do anything about it until my military stint was over for the year."

"And now it is?" Rachel's voice shook despite her efforts to keep it steady.

"Yes. I'm on my way back to Montreux right now and will be getting off the train in a few minutes. Alain will be waiting for me. Be assured I will have a frank discussion with him about why it was wrong to take matters into his own hands."

"No—" she cried out.

"No, what?" he demanded with a ring of authority in his voice reminiscent of the younger Tris who'd exhibited a powerful personality even back then.

She moistened her lips nervously. "I asked him not to tell you. He promised it would be our secret. Since he kept his end of the bargain, please don't say anything to him about it."

"Why did you feel you had to swear him to silence?"

Her heart jammed into her ribs. "I was very touched that he loves you so much, he wanted me to help you fill in the blanks of your memory. But I told him that it should have been you who called me if you felt the need. Since you hadn't done that, I thought it best to forget the whole thing."

"You did an effective job of getting through to him," he murmured, increasing her guilt. "Aside from the fact that I don't approve of what he did, I find your reaction even more curious."

Her eyes closed tightly. "I don't know what you mean."

"If we were simply two college students who enjoyed each other's company aboard ship, I'm interested to find out why you're so frightened, you couldn't be open about it with my nephew."

"Frightened?" Perspiration beaded her hairline.

"Yes. Shall I tell you about my conversation with Madame Soulis, the directrice of your school in Geneve? According to her you became ill and had to leave Grand-Chene after only a few months."

He knew.

Rachel almost collapsed.

Tris was no ordinary man. His genius was apparent whether he was captain of his hockey team, or head of a multimillion dollar family business.

The Monbrisson name was renowned throughout Europe, all because of his instincts which made him a force to contend with in the corporate world. He would never let this go now.

"Tris? You've caught me as I was walking out the door to work. I'm afraid this isn't a good time for the kind of discussion you want to have. If you cou—"

"Don't let me keep you," he interrupted her. "The next time we talk, it'll be in person," he declared, sending a frisson of alarm through her body.

"No—please—" she cried, needing space to think, but he wasn't giving her any.

"That's the second time I've heard pure terror in your voice."

Ignoring his astute observation she said, "No one deserves closure more than you do. I'm so sorry about your terrible accident, and I would be happy to meet you somewhere to answer any questions you have."

"I'll make this easy for you and see you at your house tonight."

She groaned inwardly. There was no stopping him. "I-I have plans for this evening. If you could wait until tomorrow, I'll take time off from work."

"*Bien.* I'll be in Concord this evening and will call you to make final arrangements. *A bientot, Rachel.*"

"Uncle Tris!"

As Tris stepped off the train, his nephew came flying. They gave each other a bear hug.

"Where are your grandparents?"

"In the car at the back of the station."

"Good. Why don't we get a drink before we join them? I'm thirsty."

"So am I. It's been hot for the last few days."

"It was warm where I was, too."

They made their way inside the *gare* to the food counter. Tris bought them two sodas. They wandered over by the windows away from everyone else to drink them.

"I'm glad you're back."

"So am I, but I'm afraid I'm going to have to leave again for a few more days. That's what I wanted to talk to you about."

A pained expression broke out on Alain's face. "When do you have to go?"

"As soon as I can change clothes and pack a bag."

"Did Guy say there's an emergency at one of the hotels?"

"No. I'm flying to New Hampshire to meet Rachel Marsden."

The bottle almost fell out of his nephew's hand. "You are?"

"Yes. I phoned her a little while ago. She's expecting me tonight."

His nephew suddenly averted his eyes, the telltale sign of his guilt. "Did she tell you I called her?" Alain asked, working the toe of his sandal against the floor.

Tris drained his bottle and put it in the receptacle. Alain followed suit. "Not exactly. She thought I was phoning because you'd broken your promise to her."

Alain's head reared. His eyes looked suspiciously bright. "I wouldn't have."

He tousled his nephew's hair. "I know that. What I don't understand is why the *directrice* of the school didn't tell me you'd phoned her wanting the same information?"

A resigned sigh escaped Alain's lips. "Guy got it for me from the school receptionist."

His nephew was not only determined, but resourceful. "So...now my assistant is in on this, too."

"Yes, but he swore he would never say anything."

"He kept his promise." When Tris had phoned Guy for an update on business, his assistant had been mum on the subject of Alain.

"Are you mad at me?"

"No. I think I'm very lucky to have a nephew who would go to the lengths you did to help me remember my past."

Alain's relief was visible. "Ms. Marsden asked me to leave it alone."

"Do you know why?"

"She said something kind of weird."

"What was that?"

"I shouldn't wake up a dog if it's sleeping." He cocked his head. "What did she mean?"

"Can't you guess?"

His eyes squinted up at him. "Because it might make it mad for being bothered?"

"That's one way of putting it."

"But you're not mad."

If only Alain knew... So many destructive emotions were bombarding Tris, he couldn't put a name to them.

"Let's just say that now I've talked to her, I'm anxious to meet her and clear up some questions I've had." He put a hand on Alain's shoulder. "Come on. The grandparents will be wondering what's keeping us."

"Wait—"

"What is it?"

"You were right about one thing."

"What's that?"

"You know how Rachel promised there'd never be anyone else for her but you?"

"I remember."

"Well, she broke it just like you said she would."

"You mean she's married."

"I guess she already told you. She has a daughter, too." He kept on chatting. "Her name's

Natalie. She's the one who answered the phone when I called."

Tris felt the impact of his nephew's words like the grenade that had exploded a little too near him during one of the mock raids.

Mon Dieu.

Ever since Alain had read him the note, he'd been plagued by a sense of unease where his relationship with Rachel Marsden had been concerned. Since speaking with Madame Soulis, he'd entertained certain suspicions.

After talking to Rachel, he was in no doubt.

He'd made her pregnant.

Why else had she been so desperate to keep things hushed up.

Was Natalie his flesh and blood?

Rachel could have had several children by now. If his child were alive, the eldest would be Tris's son or daughter.

Then again, she might have given up their baby for adoption, or miscarried…or heaven forbid, ended her pregnancy. Whatever the answer, he could scarcely comprehend it.

"Uncle Tris? Are you all right?"

"Of course," he lied. "I'm just anxious to leave for the States so I can meet Rachel Marsden and get filled in on my past."

"I wish I could go with you."

He grimaced. "I wish it were possible, but this is something I have to do alone."

"I know. I'm glad you're going to find out what happened. Maybe then your headaches will go away."

Tris repressed a groan and hugged his nephew.

"I swear I'll be back in time to take you camping tomorrow afternoon. For the time being, I'll tell your grandparents some unexpected business has come up I have to deal with."

"Okay."

Before they went out to his parents' car, he phoned his pilot in Geneva and told him to get the jet ready for takeoff.

CHAPTER THREE

By the time Natalie and Kendra came running out the doors of the ice rink to the car, Rachel was an emotional disaster.

"Hi, Mom!"

"Hi, Mrs. Marsden!"

Both girls put their bags in the trunk, then got in the back seat.

"How was practice?" Rachel asked as she drove out of the parking lot.

To her relief they regaled her with enough information that they were still talking about it when she pulled in Pearsolls' driveway a few minutes later to let Kendra out.

Once she'd retrieved her bag and had run in the house, Rachel started up the car again. To her chagrin, her precocious daughter eyed her with concern. "What's wrong, Mom? You're so quiet. Is Nana sick or something?"

"No. This isn't about your grandmother." There was no easy way to broach the subject. Once they reached the street and merged with the traffic Rachel said, "Your father called me this morning after you left for Kendra's house."

Natalie stared at her incredulously. "On his own? I mean, Alain didn't tell him to call?"

"No." Rachel was still in shock. In fact she'd been in this condition all day, and had gone home from work early. "No one told him to do anything. He made it abundantly clear he was acting independent of his nephew."

"Oh, Mom—"

"He'll be in Concord tonight."

"You're kidding—" The joy in her daughter's voice was beyond description. "Does he know about me?"

He knows.

"Not about you specifically, honey. He hung up before we could have a long conversation. But I can tell he suspects we had a child together, and he won't rest until he discovers the truth for himself.

"That's why he decided to fly here immediately. I told him to call the house this evening and I'd make arrangements to meet him tomorrow."

"Why can't we meet him tonight?"

"For one thing, it may be too late. For another, you and I need a little time to talk about this and what it's going to mean."

"What do we have to talk about?"

"I'm sure he's married and has a family. Finding out he has a daughter will change his life as much as it'll change yours."

"Do you think he won't love me as much as he loves his other kids?"

"Of course he will. But that's not the point, honey. Meeting you is going to transform his world. And your existence will come as a huge surprise to his wife and children, not to mention his parents and his brother's family."

"But he's my father, too!"

"Of course. The fact that he's made the decision to see us as soon as possible means he does care. That sounds like the Tris I once knew, and it's obvious to me he hasn't changed in that regard even if that portion of his life is a blank. But we have to discuss how this is going to impact all of us."

"You're talking about visitation. I mean, if he wants to go on seeing me."

"Yes."

"You think he won't?"

The tremor in her voice made Rachel want to

reach over and crush her daughter to her, but she couldn't do that until they arrived at the house.

"Honey? Right now he doesn't know positively we had a baby together. That's why he's coming. To find out.

"I'm sure a lot of possibilities are going through his head. Before we make any assumptions, we have to wait until you two have met and we've talked this through.

"Don't forget you and your father live on two different continents. The situation isn't like your friend Molly's. She can spend every other weekend at her dad's house because it's only a mile away from her mother's."

Natalie's chin trembled. "You're just saying these things because you don't think he's going to want a relationship with me, huh."

Rachel pulled the car up in front of their townhouse and turned off the engine. Eyeing her daughter she said, "I'm your mom and love you more than life itself. I'm trying to be as honest with you as I can.

"The truth is, I don't know what he'll think when he finds out he has a child. My greatest concern is to keep you from being hurt, but it isn't possible to shield you from everything."

Her daughter's pained expression was the

last thing she saw before Natalie opened the passenger door. She grabbed her things from the back seat and ran inside the house.

After locking the car, Rachel followed, but her heart was so heavy she felt like her body weighed a thousand pounds.

The second she stepped in the living room, the house phone rang. She almost jumped out of her skin before hurrying into the kitchen to get it.

Natalie had beaten her to it. Her brows furrowed before she put her hand over the mouthpiece.

"It's Steve," she whispered. "He's worried because you weren't at work and haven't been answering your cell phone. Please call him back on it. I want to keep our phone free in case *my* father calls."

Rachel took the phone from her and apologized to Steve for not calling him earlier. She told him something important had come up and she would call him back in a little while on her cell phone.

Not two seconds after Rachel had replaced the receiver, it rang again. She picked up immediately, thinking maybe he'd tried to tell her something vital and she'd cut him off too soon.

"Steve?"

"Afraid not. *Bonsoir, Rachel.*"

Her breath caught. "Tris—I—I wasn't expecting you to phone for another couple of hours at least."

Natalie was right there and knew her father was on the other end of the phone. Rachel could tell her daughter was so excited and nervous at the same time, she was practically dancing on the spot.

"I'm parked across the street. I take it that was my daughter Natalie I saw run in your house just now. She'd be the right age. From a distance she has the look of my mother."

A moan escaped Rachel's throat. Evidently he'd had a conversation with his nephew since phoning her. "Yes."

There was a palpable silence. "Does she know who I am?" his voice grated.

"Yes."

After she heard his sharp intake of breath he said, "Does your husband know I'm her father?"

Rachel trembled. "I-I'm not married yet."

After a tension-filled pause, "Alain thought you were. So what are you saying? Are you engaged to this Steve? Living with him?"

No. Not even close.

She wheeled away from Natalie's probing glance. It was uncanny how much he sounded so much like the old, decisive Tris who was a natural born leader and refused to let anything get in the way of what he wanted.

"No."

"Then you and Natalie are alone right now?"

"Yes, but—"

"I'm coming in."

He clicked off before she could beg him not to.

Tris was angry.

It was a deep, profound anger. The kind that would make it difficult, if not impossible, for him to forgive her for her silence all these years.

Frightened in a brand-new way, Rachel put the phone back on the hook.

Natalie pulled on her arm. "When am I going to see him?"

Help.

"Right now. He's walking up to the front door."

Just then the doorbell rang.

"Oh my gosh— He knows who I am, huh."

"Yes."

"Can I answer it? Please?"

Her daughter's beautiful dark brown eyes,

so much like Tris's, shone with a luster she'd never seen before.

"Go ahead," she said through wooden lips.

Ever since Rachel had learned about Alain's phone call, she'd had the presentiment that their lives would be thrown into chaos, never to be the same again.

With one unexpected turn of events, her carefully orchestrated life with Natalie had been caught up in a whirlwind by forces she'd couldn't combat or control.

She had no choice but to be carried to another place. Until it blew itself out, no one could predict the amount of destruction it would wreak.

Tracing her daughter's footsteps, Rachel reached the end of the hall leading into the living room. She hung back as Natalie opened the front door, so she could still witness what was happening.

When she saw the tall, spectacular looking man standing on the threshold, the sight of him reduced her limbs to water.

It was Tris. But over the last twelve years, the good-looking nineteen-year-old heartthrob she'd fallen in love with had changed into the most gorgeous man she'd ever seen in her life.

His hair was more black than brown. He

wore it shorter than he'd done in his early college days. Natalie had inherited his coloring and height.

He had a straight nose which he'd also bequeathed to their daughter. But where her chin was softly rounded like Rachel's, he possessed a firm jaw and a cleft in his she'd always loved to touch and kiss.

Unlike the jeans and polo shirts he'd worn on the ship, he was dressed in an expensive looking gray suit. The combination of his silk tie with its various shades of charcoal, silver and gray toned with his white shirt, dazzled Rachel's eyes.

At a glance his whole demeanor proclaimed him the successful, wealthy hotelier of the prominent Monbrisson family.

As Rachel took in everything from the distance, she watched father and daughter studying each other with the same searching intensity. Since opening the door, Natalie had been speechless. With good reason.

No father in Concord or anywhere else had his powerful physique or striking masculine features. He spoke first.

"I always wanted a daughter. You're so beautiful, Natalie, I can hardly find the words." His low voice sounded husky.

"I always wanted my dad," she answered in a tear-filled voice.

"Then how about a hug."

Rachel's eyes blurred as she watched him crush their daughter in his strong arms. He picked her up and rocked her, causing her dark ponytail to swing back and forth. The contrast between his elegance and the T-shirt and shorts she'd worn to hockey practice made the picture even more poignant.

Natalie's quiet sobs of joy were interspersed by endearments he spoke to her in French, forcing Rachel to look away.

Though she couldn't help but be thankful Tris was showing Natalie the unqualified acceptance she craved from a father, another part of Rachel's soul was horrified to realize that she'd kept them apart all these years.

Just the way Tris communed with his daughter as they quietly picked out the similarities in each other, Rachel realized he would never accept her reasons for failing to look him up in Montreux.

Not telling him he was going to be a father after she'd returned home and gone to the doctor was the most terrible mistake she'd ever made in her life.

He would see the last twelve years as wasted time he could never get back or recapture with his daughter. He wouldn't buy any explanation of Rachel's.

Tris isn't going to forgive me.

As that reality crept over her, she started to shake uncontrollably. Just then the phone rang again. Steve— She hadn't called him back yet. Though they didn't have a date until tomorrow night, naturally he was wondering if something was wrong.

Rachel hurried to the kitchen to answer it. Much as she didn't want to hurt Steve's feelings, she would have to tell him the truth, that Natalie's father had shown up and she couldn't talk right now. She would have to call him tomorrow.

Heaven help her, but Tris was back in her life in a way she could never have imagined.

Tris studied his adorable dark-haired daughter who was examining him with her heart in her eyes.

"How do you say 'Dad' in French?"

"Papa."

"That sounds like grandpa. Can I just call you Dad?"

Delighted and moved by her desire to acknowledge him as her father, he said, "There's nothing I want more."

He was rewarded with a glowing smile. "I have a present for you, Dad. Just a second while I get it. Don't go away!"

"I came here to see you, *ma fille*. I'm not going anywhere else."

Her lovely brown eyes set in that appealing eleven- year-old face filled with tears again. "I'm so glad. What does *fille* mean?"

He had to clear his throat. "My precious daughter."

She gave him another strong hug before her long legs disappeared up the stairs. Once again he was struck by her remarkable resemblance to the family, his mother in particular.

His parents weren't going to believe it. Once they got over the shock, they would adore their granddaughter who exuded a rare sweetness and vulnerability. Come to think of it, those were some of the qualities he admired in Alain.

She would help fill that hole in his parents' hearts left when Bernard and Francoise died.

Already Tris loved her with an intensity he didn't know himself capable of. The spontaneity of her love, her complete openness and generosity of spirit had overwhelmed him.

He hadn't yet spoken to the blond woman who'd chosen not to make an appearance yet. Tris could only guess why she'd decided to stay out of sight.

Undoubtedly her guilt in keeping Natalie a secret from him all these years was the primary reason he'd been given the chance to be alone with his daughter for a little while.

But he wasn't complaining. By the two of them getting acquainted on their own, there'd been no awkwardness. The bonding that had just taken place was extraordinary, almost as if he'd always known his daughter.

While he waited for Natalie to come back, he looked around the cozy living room filled with shelves of books and some framed prints of his favorite Impressionists.

He liked the combination of comfortable brown leather furnishings and glass tables with flowering plants. An oriental rug covered the hardwood floors. Whatever else he thought about Rachel Marsden, he had to admit she'd created a lovely home full of warmth and character for their offspring.

"Here—" Natalie reappeared and ran over to him, handing him something. "Does this look familiar?"

Incroyable. His old hockey ring.

"I'll say it does. My team was called the Montreux Meteors."

"That's what Mom told me."

His mind reeled. All these years Rachel had kept Natalie a secret from him. He couldn't comprehend it.

"After we won the pro tournament at the end of the season, we were presented these rings. It wasn't until after I went home from the hospital that I realized it was missing from my finger.

"I thought I'd left it because jewelry is always removed before surgery. But when I inquired later, they said I hadn't been wearing a ring."

"Mom said you gave it to her as a promise ring until you could buy her an engagement ring. She said you were going to take her shopping for one after your training camp was over."

Another groan escaped. He rubbed his thumb over the raised letters that spelled out Meteors. A stylized hockey stick formed the *T.*

Natalie's mother had memories of the night he'd given this to her. But he couldn't share in them. All he could do was marvel that the fruit of their undoubtedly passionate union was standing in front of him.

His gaze flicked to Natalie. As he continued

to study his daughter, he realized her smile, the shape of her face and lips, were physical traits that had to belong to her mother, the woman he'd made love to twelve years ago.

She must have been exceptional for him to fall so hard. But the fact that she'd kept all knowledge of their daughter from him revealed a serious character flaw in her nature. He ground his teeth in an effort to tamp down his fury.

The important thing here was to get acquainted with his flesh and blood first. Recriminations would be pointless.

But as Rachel Marsden would come to find out, there was going to be a price to pay for her sin of omission.

Suddenly Tris sensed he and Natalie weren't alone.

He looked beyond her to the stunning woman with shoulder length ash blond hair who'd just entered the living room. Of medium height, she exuded the beguiling femininity he'd caught glimpses of in his adolescent daughter.

Even from the distance separating them, he could see her dark lashed eyes were an incredible translucent green.

Helpless to do otherwise, his gaze traveled

over her high-boned cheeks and wide, full mouth. It finally dropped to her slender yet rounded figure not quite hidden beneath the classy pastel blue suit she was wearing.

His pulse throbbed wildly in his throat and temple, a sensation that hadn't happened for so long, he couldn't remember the last time.

He resented this initial gut reaction to her, but attributed it to the fact that he'd been inordinately curious about the mother of his child who anyone could see was growing into a real beauty herself.

"I gave your ring to Natalie before she started school," Rachel began in that almost breathless voice he'd heard on the phone. "I wanted her to know something special about her father that was interesting and uniquely you."

"Yup," Natalie chimed in. "I thought it was so cool my dad was a professional ice hockey player. That's the reason *I* wanted to play it too. But I had to wait until I turned ten."

"You play hockey now?" Tris murmured in a bemused state.

Natalie nodded. "Mom just picked me up from practice."

"She's your daughter," Rachel inserted. "You'll be proud to know the coach thinks she's so talented, he gave her the position of left wing. Because of her fearlessness, she helped their team win the regional Peewees championship last season."

"Do you still play, Dad?"

"Not since my accident. Do you love it?"

"Yes! My team's called the Concord Cavalry," Natalie informed him with a broad smile. "Tomorrow's our first practice game before fall season starts. Will you come and watch me play? We rock!"

For a moment Tris feared this was some kind of fantastic dream from which he would awaken and find himself alone and desolate. Feeling Natalie's arms go around him had completely changed his life.

He watched Rachel put protective hands on their daughter's shoulders. "Honey? Your father just got here. We have no idea what his plans are, or if he brought his wife and children with him. Why don't we all sit down to talk."

With those words, the gloves had come off.

Rachel Marsden was staking her claim. Now that he'd been allowed to see his daughter, she couldn't wait for him to announce his imminent departure from her house and the country. Undoubtedly the man she planned to marry was waiting for her to phone him with the all clear signal.

That was fine. But before Tris left, he was about to stake his own claim.

Without hesitation he pocketed the ring to give back later, then moved closer and grasped his daughter's hands, ignoring Rachel's suggestion that they sit.

Looking down into those dark brown orbs he said, "I'm not married, *cherie*."

"You're not?"

"Not yet," he mimicked Rachel's earlier admission. "And now that I know I have a daughter, I want you to come to Switzerland and live with me."

"You mean it?" she blurted joyously.

"How can you doubt it? Because of my amnesia, we've lost out on eleven years of a father-daughter relationship. I don't want to miss another day."

"Neither do I," she confessed. "I always thought my friends were so lucky to grow up with their dads."

Emotion caused him to squeeze her hands a little tighter. He kissed the top of her head.

"If I'd known about you, we'd have been a family from the beginning."

Out of the periphery he noticed her mother's face lose color. It pleased him no end to watch her writhe in guilt.

"Let me tell you about my house, *ma fille*. It's a chalet that sits on a lush green mountain top in Caux overlooking Lake Geneva. Along the shore below is a castle, and you can see across the water to the French Alps. There's a lake paddle steamer to take you to Geneva where you can visit your mother's old school."

Natalie jumped in place. "Mom told me we would travel there one day so I could see where she studied."

"That day is here." Taking advantage of Rachel's shocked silence he said, "Whenever you feel like it, you can walk down the mountain to your grandparents' house in Montreux. They'll be overjoyed to learn they've got a beautiful granddaughter."

"Do you think they'll like me?"

"They'll adore you," he murmured emotionally. "So will your cousin Alain. He lives with me."

"How come?"

"His parents were killed in a car crash a year ago."

"Both Bernard and Francoise?" Rachel cried in a stricken voice.

It shouldn't have surprised him she remembered the names of his brother and sister-in-law. But he marveled that she sounded like it mattered to her what had happened to them.

He grimaced. "The tragedy has been very difficult for the family, but especially for Alain. I love him as if he were my own son. He's quite remarkable."

In fact if it hadn't been for his nephew's inquisitive nature, that note might have stayed unread forever. Certainly Tris wouldn't be united with the daughter he hadn't known existed until now.

Rachel looked stricken. "I remember the pictures you showed me of them holding their new baby. That poor boy. Thank heaven he has you."

The tremor in Rachel's voice was so real, it touched him in spite of his anger that she hadn't once tried to find out why he'd never called her or written to her again.

She was a total enigma to him.

"How old is he, Dad?"

"Twelve."

"Just a year older than me."

Tris glanced at his daughter. "You're practically twins."

"He was really nice on the phone," Natalie added.

"With the help of him and his friends, you'll be speaking fluent French around our house in no time."

"I was planning to take it at school this fall."

"*Bon.* That'll make it easier when you join the girls' ice hockey team in Montreux. You'll be happy to know they have a new ice rink. One of my old hockey buddies is the coach for the school age kids. They need a good left wing."

"Oh my gosh—Mom—did you hear that?" Her head whipped around to look up at her mother.

But Rachel's demeanor had undergone a change. Her eyes were impaling his like green lasers.

"I heard."

She was getting ready to send their daughter upstairs out of hearing distance. Before that happened he needed to make his move.

"Once upon a time you agreed to marry me," Tris asserted bluntly. "Though I don't remember that period of my life, I have your letter and the ring to prove we were planning our wedding."

"That was a long time ago."

"True. But the fact remains we now have a daughter who needs both of us. I want her in my life on a permanent basis," he declared as if they were alone in the room.

"Oh, Mom—"

He smiled at his ecstatic daughter.

Rachel shook her head wildly. "Honey? I— I need to talk to your father in private."

"I'd like her to stay," Tris countermanded.

"Please don't make this any more difficult than it is."

"Don't you think there've been enough secrets?" he fired back. "I realize you're in love with another man. This places *our* daughter in the middle of an untenable situation.

"Since we know she won't be happy away from you or me, then I suggest you move to Switzerland with Natalie while we all get acquainted. I'm thinking a year."

"Could we, Mom?" his daughter implored.

"My house has plenty of room for your boyfriend and your parents."

"There's just my nana," Natalie informed him wistfully. "My grandpa died two years ago."

"I'm sorry you lost him, *petite.* Your nana can

come and live with us if she wants. For that matter, the invitation includes any of your friends who might like to ski with us at Christmas and Easter."

Natalie let out a yelp. "Kendra will die when I tell her!"

He smiled at his daughter. "I take it she's your best friend."

"Yes. She plays hockey, too!"

His gaze flicked back to Rachel who'd gone distinctly pale. "As for your job, whatever it is," he continued in the same vein, "I'm sure that when they understand the situation, they'll give you a year's sabbatical."

"Mom works for an advertising agency," Natalie supplied proudly.

Fascinated by that piece of information he said, "There's always the need for a good one no matter where you live."

Already prepared for Rachel's outright refusal of what he'd proposed, he added the linchpin. "If you can't bring yourself to be uprooted for a year, then Alain and I will move here. I noticed there's a townhouse for sale two doors down. That way Natalie won't have to be torn between us."

"You *can't* move here—" Rachel sounded aghast.

He enjoyed watching her squirm. "Why not?"

"Aside from the obvious fact that Switzerland's your home, you have huge responsibilities."

"How do you know?"

"Because you once told me you would end up working in the family business."

Her response sounded logical. But he'd heard a slight hesitation before she answered. He wondered at the reason for it.

"I thought I'd made it clear I'll do whatever it takes to be with my daughter. For several years I've considered expanding the business beyond Europe. Why not start in Concord?"

Natalie turned to her mother. "I'd rather go to Switzerland. If Dad hadn't gotten amnesia, that's where we'd be living."

"But he *did* have that accident, honey."

Tris could tell Rachel was trembling. To his satisfaction, Natalie didn't appear to notice or be listening.

In the next instant she hugged him around the waist with surprising strength. "I'm so glad you're okay now, Dad!"

"I'm even more thankful I have a daughter. Now that we've found each other, we'll have the rest of our lives to be together. But your mother has a point. You weren't born in Switzerland, and you may not feel like it could be home to you. So I have another suggestion until we've worked out a permanent solution."

"What is it?"

"Why don't you both come for a vacation? I'll pay for everything. It's my right as your father after all. You'll be able to meet your grandparents, check out the area. See what you think. Maybe you'll decide you'd rather live where you've been raised."

"Could we come tomorrow?" She hadn't heard anything else he'd said. That was fine with him.

"I wish it were possible," he said before Rachel could protest. "But if you don't have a passport, you'll need to apply for one first. If you put a rush on it, they might arrive within a week. In the meantime you can start getting packed."

He could hear her mind absorbing everything. As for her mother, Rachel had been ready to throw him out long before now. "Since the two of you have a lot to talk over, I'm going to leave."

"Could I come to your hotel with you?"

"I'm sorry, *petite,* but I'm headed for the airport."

"How come?" she cried in panic.

"I've been away from business for the last two weeks and need to get back to Montreux." He'd made a promise to Alain and couldn't disappoint him.

Natalie didn't look the least bit happy with the news. "I was hoping you'd be able to watch my game tomorrow. I wanted my friends to meet you and everything."

"Don't worry. It's all going to happen whether we live here or in Switzerland. Before long I'll be attending all your hockey matches with Alain. Expect a call from me tomorrow night. I'll want to know how it went."

"Okay, but I wish you didn't have to go." She sounded a lot like Alain just then.

As they hugged one more time, Tris got a perverse thrill out of seeing the turbulence in a pair of stormy green eyes staring at him in pain and rage.

Join the club.

CHAPTER FOUR

RACHEL watched him disappear out the door.

He came, he saw, he conquered, she thought hysterically. Tris had won the war by the divine right of fatherhood.

Without waging any kind of battle, he'd simply laid down the terms of surrender. She could live in his home for a year where Natalie would be totally won over and never want to leave him.

If that proposal wasn't acceptable, he would make his home in Concord, two doors away from them.

Either of the above would fulfill their daughter's dreams.

How shrewd he was.

He knew normal visitation wasn't to be considered. Natalie wanted her father with every particle of her being, but she would never be able to stand living apart from Rachel. By calling on all of his wisdom, he'd thought up the perfect solution without having to wage a custody battle Rachel would lose.

Whatever was decided, he would get what he wanted and Natalie's world would be complete. Never mind that Rachel's life would forever be conflicted.

"Mom?" The pleading in her daughter's eyes haunted her. "Can we send for our passports after my game tomorrow?"

"The passport office won't be open until Monday."

"What are you thinking?"

She took a steadying breath. "I'm thinking that your father hasn't changed one iota from the younger man he once was. He's a fighter. Now that he knows he has a daughter, he wants you in his life."

"He's invited you to stay with us, Mom."

Stay with us?

Like her father, Natalie concluded that the shortest distance between two points was a straight line, period. In her daughter's mind she was already living in Switzerland with Tris on that lush green mountaintop overlooking *Lac Leman*.

In theory the plan was perfect. Rachel couldn't

fault it. A strangled sound escaped her throat. "It's not that simple, honey."

"I know," she said, sounding very grown up just then. "Did you tell Steve that Dad's here in Concord?"

"Yes."

"I bet he was upset when he found out."

"I think surprised would be a better word." Rachel was the one upset, alarmed, shocked. What if she never recovered? That's what was terrifying her.

"Now that you've seen Dad, do you still love him?"

Oh, Natalie...

"You said you could never love another man the way you once loved my father."

"Honey—" Rachel was trying frantically to make sense of her chaotic emotions. "I cherish Tris's memory, but I'm not in love with him now. There's an old saying that love has to be fed.

"We've been apart twelve years. I'm a different person than I once was. So is he. I have no doubts he's involved with someone else. And don't forget—he's raising his nephew."

"He still invited us to live with him," Natalie persisted. "Dad told you Steve could come and visit whenever he wanted."

Tris had known exactly what he was doing

when he'd insisted Natalie remain downstairs to hear everything.

Rachel struggled for breath. "That's ridiculous. For one thing, Steve's a busy man with an insurance business to run, honey. For another, he would never stay in your father's home."

A hurt look broke out on her face. "Dad was just trying to be nice and make it easier for you, Mom."

Pain ripped Rachel's heart apart. Natalie didn't have a clue about the man who ran the Monbrisson empire. She was too blinded with joy over being loved and claimed by her long lost father to understand the tactics he'd used to create this monumental upheaval in their lives.

"Natalie—you have to understand your father's angry with me because I never tried to look him up and let him know about you."

"How come you didn't?"

"You know why. I told you the reason a long time ago." She expelled the breath she'd been holding. "But maybe you're finally old enough to understand, so I'll explain it again.

"After two months of not hearing from him, I believed I'd only been a girl he'd had fun with on the ship, nothing more.

"No woman wants to beg a man for his love.

If he doesn't want to be with her of his own free will, then it's pointless. That's the way I felt.

"The trouble is, I'd fallen in love and had made the mistake of sleeping with him when I knew better. I thought we'd be together forever. Getting in touch with him after you were born to tell him he had a child wouldn't have made him love me. Just the opposite in fact.

"He was a professional ice hockey player with dreams of rising to the top. I was afraid that because he lived in Switzerland and we lived here, you'd only get to see him once a year, if at all. My only thought was to protect you from being hurt. I thought it best that we went it alone. Can't you see that?"

She averted her eyes. "Yes."

"Look—I don't blame him for being upset right now. Tris has just found out he has a daughter. It's obvious he's prepared to do anything to make you a part of his life.

"But my living in his house is out of the question. As for him uprooting his life to move to New Hampshire—well, it—it's absolutely ludicrous."

"What does ludicrous mean?"

"Crazy!" she said for want of a better word.

"Why?"

Rachel hugged her arms to her waist. "There's a lot I haven't told you about him."

"Like what?"

"You would have to see where he comes from to begin to understand."

"What do you mean?"

"You've heard of the French Riviera and Monte Carlo where a lot of movie stars and royals live and vacation in the South of France?"

Natalie nodded.

"Well, Montreux is like Monte Carlo, full of palaces, yachts, movie stars and royals. People call that part of Lake Geneva the Swiss Riviera of Europe. You need a fortune to even vacation in such a fabulous place.

"Your father's family has lived there for generations. They're prominent and wealthy. With his brother gone, and his father getting older, Tris has the weight of the company on his shoulders."

Natalie squinted up at her. "What company?"

"They're hoteliers. If you want to know just how important a figure your father is, type in the name Monbrisson Hotels on the Internet. When you see the results, you'll begin to get an idea of what I'm telling you."

In a lightning move, Natalie bounded up the

stairs to the third bedroom they'd made into a study. Rachel followed.

Her daughter was a whiz on the computer and could navigate the various search engines without problem.

After a few minutes Rachel heard, "Oh my gosh—"

She moved behind her daughter. Putting her hands on her shoulders, she leaned over to look at the screen with her. Each hotel had been a former palace. All were different and luxurious.

"Your father's the one responsible for the expansion beyond Switzerland."

Natalie turned her head. "How do you know?"

"Because I've checked this Web site now and again, wondering whether I dared call him to tell him about you. There's a business profile of him, plus pictures of your grandfather and former Monbrissons. You can click on it from the home page.

"A year ago I came close to phoning his office, but at the last minute I hung up because I didn't know how he would react when he heard the news. I guess I didn't want to go through the pain of finding out in case you could be hurt."

Natalie brought up the article on her father. The picture of him was several years old. He looked more like the younger Tris. Since then, sorrow over his brother's death had added lines to his arresting features.

"I'm glad he called you on his own," her daughter declared. "Now I know he really loves me and wants me." She turned in the swivel chair. "I want to live with him, Mom, but I want us to all be together. Can we go there for a vacation like he said?"

Rachel straightened, knowing what she had to do. "Once our passports arrive, we'll fly over there for a week."

"But—"

"It's all I can promise," Rachel broke in. "I can't just leave my job without making arrangements."

"Steve will have a cow when he meets him."

Rachel groaned because she'd forgotten all about Steve. It was as if he'd never existed. "What do you mean?"

"Mom—" Natalie rolled her eyes. "Kendra and her mother will die when they get a look at Dad. All my friends are going to be so jealous! I've got to call her and tell her what's happened!" She reached for the receiver.

"Natalie—"

"I know. I won't say anything about our plans. All I want to do is tell her I met my father and he loves me the way her dad loves her."

Emotion swamped Rachel so she couldn't talk. After giving her daughter a resigned nod, she went downstairs to get her cell phone out of her purse.

Like feathers from a pillow being lost in the wind, Rachel felt the careful world she'd constructed had just blown apart, never to be put back together again.

When she heard her mother's voice on the end of the phone, all she could say was "Mom—" before she broke down sobbing.

"What's the matter, darling?"

Rachel sank down on the couch. It took a few minutes to get herself under control before she told her everything. When she'd finished, she said, "I honestly don't know what to do."

"Natalie has always been your first priority, so of course you know what to do. He's asking for your help to establish a relationship with his daughter. Naturally he needs you there. Otherwise it won't work. I must say I admire the way he's handling this. It takes a real man to acknowledge what has happened and want Natalie in his life."

She closed her eyes tightly. "He's angry, Mom."

"I would be, too."

"You think I'm horrible for never telling him, don't you."

"Rachel Marsden. You know me better than that. Once upon a time I was eighteen years old without the vision to understand anything but my own pain.

"If your father had asked me to marry him after only knowing me ten days, and then he'd disappeared from my life, I'm quite sure I would have done exactly what you did and raised the baby by myself. You've been a remarkable mother, darling. Your father and I have always been very proud of you."

"I could never have survived without your love and support, Mom. Thank you. Thank you for all you've done for me. All you still do," she whispered. The tears dripped off her chin.

"You don't need to thank me. Now that Tris knows about Natalie, let him shoulder some of the responsibility. Obviously he wants to. It will help dissipate his pain for all the years he missed being a father to her. As his nephew Alain told you, it might help cure his residue headaches from the accident.

"In time I'm convinced he'll let go of his anger. But if you fight him, you risk injuring your relationship with Natalie. That would be the real tragedy."

She sniffed. "You're right."

"Take your father's advice. Don't try to solve everything all at once. Remember his favorite movie about the psychiatrist who wrote a book called *Baby Steps?*"

It was Rachel's favorite film, too. She let out a laugh in spite of her pain. "I remember. It's hilarious."

"The title's instructive," her mother reminded her.

"There's just one problem. I don't like leaving you."

"Good heavens—I hope that's not true! I have my own life, darling. This is going to be a real vacation for you and Natalie. Enjoy it and stop worrying about me. There is such a thing as the phone."

"I know, but—"

"No buts. Think of what this is going to mean to Natalie."

"Mom?"

Rachel raised her head in time to see Natalie race down the stairs toward her. The stars in her eyes said it all.

"I'm on the phone with Nana, honey."

"Can I talk to her?"

"Of course. Go ahead." She handed it to her.

"Does Nana know about Dad?" she whispered.

"Yes."

A smile broke out on Natalie's face. "Guess what?"

"What?"

"Kendra looked up Dad's picture on the Internet and croaked!"

The Fasten Seat Belts sign went on.

"Oh my gosh, Mom!" Natalie cried a few minutes later as Tris's private jet started making its descent. "Is that Lake Geneva?"

"Yes, and there's Mount Blanc in the French Alps. It's almost sixteen thousand feet high." Though it was seven in the evening Swiss time, the sun still reflected off the snowy peaks.

"It's so beautiful I can't believe it!"

The last time Rachel had seen Switzerland from this altitude, she'd been on her way home to Concord, so heartsick over Tris's defection, and so nauseated without knowing the reason why, she couldn't appreciate anything.

Today everything was different. Tris would be waiting for them at the airport. It had been ten days since Natalie had seen her father. She'd been going crazy waiting for this moment.

Though Rachel was nervous of what the future held, she knew the decision to bring Natalie to Switzerland was the right one.

Rachel had grown up with a wonderful father. Every child should be so blessed. Now it was her daughter's turn to know that same sense of belonging and security.

The Marsden family had been dominated by females for the last couple of years. What a change it would be for Natalie to feel a father's strong arms around her, and bask in his loving reassurance. There was no doubt in Rachel's mind Tris would provide all of those things for their daughter.

Even if he won't provide the same things for me.

She shivered involuntarily.

The next few minutes passed by in a blur before the jet touched down and taxied to a stop.

"Oh, Mom—I'm so excited!"

As they undid their seat belts, a customs agent came aboard. He welcomed them to Switzerland and stamped their passports.

A private jet—

Preferential treatment—

This was just the beginning of what it was going to be like to live in Tris's exclusive world for a little while. Natalie wasn't the only one enchanted by her father who appeared bigger than life. Rachel had to keep reminding herself this was her new reality.

The steward flashed Natalie a smile before escorting her to the exit. Rachel reached for her purse and followed them.

She was glad she'd worn a wrinkle-resistant outfit for the flight which had started at six-thirty this morning. The casual yellow top and white and yellow floral print skirt was summery, yet dressy enough for whatever Tris had planned.

Just before she reached the opening, she heard Natalie call out, "Dad!" When next Rachel looked, she watched her daughter go flying down the steps into her father's arms, solving the problem of levitation for all time.

He swung her around, filling the air with his deep, rich laughter. The sound thrilled Rachel to her bones. So did the sight of him in an open necked, vivid blue sport shirt and tan khakis defined by his rock-hard thighs.

She'd experienced this same breathless feeling ten days ago. It wasn't supposed to have happened again. Her pulse wasn't supposed to race this fast.

In fact she was so flustered by her reaction to him, she stumbled near the bottom of the stairs. If Tris hadn't made a lightning move to steady her, she would have fallen flat on her face. In that instant she felt his touch on her arm like a scorch mark.

"Thank you," she said in a shaky voice. "The heel of my sandal caught." When she raised her flushed face to him, she discovered his gaze taking inventory of her hair and features caught in the sun's slanting rays.

Maybe it was a trick of light but she thought she saw something flare in his dark brown eyes, reminding her of that moment on the ship when they'd first met.

She'd been told she had first sitting in the dining room at a table with some other students. When she finally found it, she realized she was late. Everyone had already started eating.

As she took her place, Tris, who was seated across from her, happened to glance up. That's when it happened. Like coming in contact with a livewire, there was this instant bolt of electricity that sizzled and burned both of them at the same moment. He stopped chewing.

Somehow she managed to sit down before she fell. By some miracle she made it through lunch, but the intense attraction between them was so overwhelming, she never quite caught her breath again.

Though it had been a decade and more, it seemed he still had that effect on her.

Out of the corner of her eye she noticed the

steward stowing their luggage in the trunk of a gleaming black Mercedes sedan parked a few yards off.

She'd seen none of these trappings with the younger Tris who'd taken time off from his rigorous hockey schedule and studies for a little adventure at sea. They were simply two students enjoying being on their own, doing the crazy little things you did at that age when you were madly in love.

Yet in that tiny slice of time, something earth-shaking had happened, with Natalie the result.

"Who wants to ride in front with me?"

"I do!" Natalie answered on cue.

"Then come on." Tris held the front and rear passenger doors open for her and Rachel. "Your grand-parents are expecting us."

He couldn't have said anything to alarm Rachel more. She'd hoped to talk privately with him before meeting his parents. No doubt his mother and father would have already condemned her for keeping news of Tris's child from ever coming to light. Rachel couldn't blame them. They didn't have the benefit of understanding her motives.

For Natalie's sake she would have to put on her best face to get through dinner, but she was dreading it.

As she climbed in the back, the luxurious leather upholstery caused her skirt to ride up, exposing one silken-clad leg. Embarrassed, she quickly tugged the material back down, but not soon enough to escape Tris's allseeing gaze.

"Where's Alain?" Natalie asked once he'd taken his place behind the wheel.

"He's helping them get dinner ready. Your grand-mere's making you something very special."

"What's her name?"

"Louise."

"That's pretty. What's my grandfather's name?"

"Marcel."

"Can I call them Grand-mere Louise and Papa Marcel?"

Tris chuckled. "They'll love it."

Before long they'd left the airport for the *centre ville*. The familiar pointed arrow French road signs brought back dozens of memories, all to do with Tris.

Natalie's head turned every which way, taking in the stately grandeur of the buildings for which the cosmopolitan city of Geneva with its *jet d'eau* was famous. She asked her father one question after another. Tris never seemed to tire of answering them.

Her natural zest for life appeared to be a constant source of pleasure to him. In Natalie's company he seemed younger, even carefree. The more father and daughter interacted so naturally, Rachel caught glimpses of the old Tris who'd displayed a fatal masculine charm even back then.

That same charisma was in evidence now, bowling over both daughter and mother. To Rachel's horror, she was helpless to do anything about it, and she'd only been in his company for a half hour.

What would happen after a whole week?

For the most part, the highway to Montreux followed the picturesque shoreline. It paralleled the tracks where a quaint red train was headed for Geneva. She could tell her daughter was hard-pressed to know whether to look at the shimmering blue water on one side of them, or the lush vineyards of the hillsides on the other.

Rachel had feasted her eyes on this fairy tale wonderland many times before, all by bus, train or lake steamer. Being chauffeured to the Monbrisson family home in Tris's luxury car was something else again.

When they reached Montreux and had pulled into a heavily wooded private drive, the sun had gone down behind the Alps. Partially hidden in the foliage was a wonderful old manor house.

It was the kind of estate her school friends had rhapsodized over from the deck of the steamer as it had pulled into the dock of Chillon castle.

At eighteen years of age, suffering from a broken heart, Rachel had viewed everything so differently back then. Her pain had been too exquisite. Montreux was Tris's home. He lived in one of those fabulous houses. The Chateau de Chillon he'd promised to show her had made up part of his playground.

But at that moment in time she hadn't been able to see anything but him, could find no joy. Rachel hadn't been able to feel anything but despair that he'd walked away from her without looking back.

Yet twelve years later, here he was sitting in front of her, his dark head and broad shoulders an imposing silhouette in the twilight.

The car rolled to a stop. At the same moment Tris shut off the purring motor, two older people and a young teenage boy emerged from the side entrance of the house. Rachel's glance happened to meet Tris's in the rearview mirror. His look of asperity left her in little doubt he viewed her as the enemy.

She felt the blood pound in her ears before

she slid out to join Natalie on the other side of the car. Tris got there first and put an arm around their daughter, urging her toward his parents.

Rachel heard their cries of delight before he said, "Maman? Papa? This is my daughter Natalie, and her mother, Rachel Marsden."

"Ma precieuse—" Louise ran to hug her granddaughter. Not even the semidarkness could hide the similarity in their coloring and body type. Tris looked like his mother which explained the resemblance.

Alain and Marcel Monbrisson were blue eyed and dark blond, though the older man's hair revealed streaks of gray. Both were tall and lanky.

Tris's father eyed Rachel for an overly long moment, but she saw no accusation in his expression before he did something surprising and kissed her on both cheeks.

"Welcome, Rachel. You've brought us a priceless gift," he said in excellent English.

Tears stung her eyes. She fought to stave them off. "Natalie's been so excited to meet her grandparents."

"We've been counting the minutes ourselves, haven't we, Alain."

Rachel looked down at Tris's solemn-faced

nephew who stood close to his grandfather. One day he would grow up to be handsome like his deceased father.

"Salut, Alain."

"Salut," he answered, looking surprised she'd said something to him in French. His eyes stared at her in apprehension.

"It looks like your uncle wanted answers to the past without anyone's help."

He nodded.

"I'm glad you called me first."

"You are?"

"It prepared me. To be honest, I'm more grateful to you than you know." She felt his relief. Without conscious thought, she reached out to give him a quick hug.

"We're all grateful to Alain."

At the sound of Tris's vibrant voice, Rachel swung around to confront him and his mother. In the background she could see Natalie in her grandfather's arms.

"Alain's our angel," Louise Monbrisson asserted, stepping forward to hug him before kissing Rachel on both cheeks. "I was so shattered by Tris's accident, I never thought to go through his backpack after the accident. I just put it away in a closet.

"After he graduated from the university and

moved into his own home in Caux, we sent everything with him including the pack. Unseen hands must have guided Alain to open it."

Unseen hands had done what Rachel should have done years earlier, but she didn't feel any animosity coming from Tris's mother. There was no rebuke in her words. For her son's sake, she would have had every reason to lash out at Rachel.

"Maman?" Tris murmured. "As you've gathered, this is the woman who wrote me that letter on the ship."

His declaration meant there were no secrets in their household. Shaken by his boldness Rachel said, "I—it's a privilege to meet you, Madame."

"Call me Louise, please—" his mother implored.

Rachel didn't see any condemnation in her eyes, either. The Monbrisson's kindness was very humbling and unexpected. "If you'll call me Rachel."

"Mais bien sur." She sounded like Tris just then, yet she spoke excellent English when she had to. Rachel could only marvel at their family's language abilities.

"Come in the house." She linked her arm through Rachel's. "After your flight, I'm sure you're anxious to refresh yourselves. I don't know how hungry you are, but I made dinner."

"We're starving, Grand-mere!" Natalie piped up from behind, causing the others to chuckle, particularly her father. It saved Rachel from having to say anything.

Though their initial warm welcome couldn't have come as a greater surprise, Rachel's emotions were still in turmoil. She hadn't had an appetite in days, and feared she wouldn't be able to do justice to the meal. Undoubtedly Louise had gone to a great deal of trouble to prepare it.

They crossed through the vestibule into a large, main floor drawing room filled with nineteenth century decor and tapestries. Beyond it she could see the dining room through some tall paneled doors. Overhead there was an ancient looking vaulted ceiling, prompting Natalie to ask if this had once been a fortress.

Tris hugged his daughter to him. "When I was a boy, I used to pretend it was. But you'll see the difference when we tour the Chateau de Chillon later on in the week."

"Mom went through that castle with her school friends."

Tris shot Rachel a dark glance. She looked away hastily, afraid to see the reproach in his eyes for having come to Montreux without trying to contact him.

But at that point in time she hadn't known she was pregnant. It wasn't until after she'd returned to the States that the reason for her flu-like symptoms became obvious.

Louise put an arm around Natalie. "Let me show you to the guest bathroom."

Though it might have been a coincidence, Rachel suspected Louise had sensed her son's tension and chose that moment to intervene. Whatever the reason, Rachel was thankful to escape his forbidding presence for a few minutes and follow his mother to the other side of the room.

Natalie appeared oblivious to the undercurrents. She was too busy marveling over her brand-new world. Rachel saw nothing in her daughter's behavior to indicate she felt any strangeness.

On the contrary, she seemed to embrace Tris's family so naturally, it was like she'd always known them. In her eagerness to rejoin them, Natalie ran out of the bathroom seconds later without hearing Rachel ask her to wait.

Left behind, she dried her hands on the towel and hurried out into the dimly lit hall, only to feel a firm hand on her arm. It was Tris who'd emerged from the shadows.

"After dinner we're going to take a drive alone. Since Natalie and Alain will want to join us, I expect your cooperation to make sure they remain with the grandparents. *Tu compris?*"

Rachel understood all right. The time for the dreaded talk wasn't far off now.

Long after they'd joined the family and had enjoyed a delicious veal dinner, she still felt his grasp in every last molecule of her body.

CHAPTER FIVE

THE pear tart dessert was quickly demolished by Natalie. Rachel could tell it pleased her grandmother no end.

"That was one of the best meals I've ever tasted," Rachel complimented her, too. "Thank you for going to so much trouble for us."

Louise beamed. "Finding out we have a granddaughter is one of the most wonderful things that's ever happened to this family."

Marcel nodded in agreement before finishing off his wine. Then he lowered his glass to the table. His body language indicated he had something serious on his mind. He eyed Rachel frankly. She got a fluttery sensation in her stomach.

"We're all anxious to know what happened when you first met Tris."

Up until now they'd plied Natalie with dozens of questions. Now it was Rachel's turn to reconstruct Tris's past to their satisfaction. She wiped her mouth with the napkin and put it down next to her dessert plate.

"My parents drove me to New York to see me off at the pier. The ship was so huge I got lost trying to find my way out on deck to wave goodbye to them.

"By the time I did, we were already sailing past the Statue of Liberty. Though it had been my idea to study abroad, it was the most lonely feeling in the world to realize the ship was headed out to sea and there was no turning back." Her voice wobbled with unexpected emotion.

Tris's piercing gaze never left hers.

She cleared her throat. "There were several students on board also traveling to Europe. I didn't know it until the steward informed me I would be eating all my meals with them at the same table. When I found it, I was late of course. Everyone was already enjoying lunch, including Tris. I have a picture."

Rachel reached in her purse for it. "I kept this photo which Natalie has seen so she would know what her father looked like. At our first meal the ship photographer went around to every table snapping pictures. You can see the people in our group including Tris and me."

She handed it to Marcel who studied it. After wiping his eyes, he passed it on to Louise.

"You're so young and happy!" she cried out. "Look, Tris. You both wore your hair longer then."

The second he took the picture from her hands, Rachel's heartbeat picked up speed. Without any show of emotion, he examined it for a long time before giving it to Alain.

Clearing her throat Rachel continued to tell them what they hungered to hear. "Tris welcomed me to the table and we started talking. After our meal, he asked me to take a walk on deck with him. It was windy, but we both loved it. While we leaned against the railing and watched the ocean, we talked about our lives, our families.

"I realized right away he loved all of you so much, and worshipped Bernard who'd become a brand-new father. He was anxious for me to meet little Alain.

"I was an only child who'd just graduated from high school, eager to study French and German in Geneva. Tris told me his family was in the hotel business which required he speak several languages fluently. He told me about his university studies in Lausanne and of course about his ice hockey.

"Growing up I did some ice skating and tennis, but I was no athlete. My father enjoyed an occasional football or basketball game on TV when he wasn't at the hospital. You can imagine I found Tris's expertise in hockey fascinating.

"During the week we were on the ship, I made him tell me all about it so I could understand the game. He was an excellent teacher. It was a good thing since I intended to go to as many of his matches as I could.

"Needless to say we spent every minute together watching films, playing quoits. At night we danced to the orchestra. Halfway across the Atlantic we ran into the outskirts of a hurricane which played havoc with the indoor swimming pool. Tris and I had more fun because the movement of the ship caused the water to move like the surf of the ocean at high tide.

"When the storm got worse, Tris stayed with me in my cabin. We weren't allowed to go up on deck. So many people were sick those last few days, but he plied me with cola and crackers to ward off seasickness. It worked.

"Because of the hurricane, we were two days late getting into Southampton. The night before we docked, he asked me to marry him. He gave me his hockey ring to wear until he could buy me an engagement ring. We planned to get married the next summer after we'd both finished another year of college.

"The next morning while we stood in line getting ready to debark, I slipped the letter inside his backpack, the one Alain found. I hoped Tris would read it later and be surprised. We took a train to the airport and flew to Geneva. Tris showed me around the city and we had a cheese fondue dinner before he said goodnight to me at the school.

"We—" Rachel's voice caught with emotion, remembering that night. She thought she would die because he had to leave her. "We made plans to meet after he'd finished his training camp in Interlaken. His intention was to take me to Montreux where we would pick out a ring and I could meet all of his family. He also wanted to show me around his hometown.

"He…promised to call me every night, and I told him I would come to his next game, wherever it was. It was the last time I saw or heard from him again," she said in a tortured whisper.

Marcel's face grew shadowed. "He called us from New York before boarding the ship. The plan was that he would phone us after he'd reached Interlaken to start his training camp."

"But the only call we received was the one

from his coach saying he'd been struck on the head the first morning of practice," Louise explained in a less than steady voice. "We were told he was lying unconscious in the hospital, to come immediately."

Suddenly Tris pushed himself away from the table and stood up. His mouth looked white around the edges.

"Now that Rachel has supplied the last piece of the puzzle, there's no need to dwell on my past any longer. If everyone will excuse us, I'm going to give her a little tour of Montreux right now."

"You two go on," Louise commented. "Marcel and I will enjoy the rest of the evening with our grandchildren."

Tris's father nodded, then began clearing the table. Natalie helped him and seemed fine with the plans. But Alain looked crushed. Not for the first time did it dawn on Rachel how hard this must be for him. He'd had his uncle all to himself since his parents' death.

"We won't be long," she assured him, but he didn't appear to be listening. She wished Tris would say something to ameliorate the situation, but his mood was no better than his nephew's.

Once they'd reached the car, Rachel was feeling distinctly worried and uncomfortable.

"Tris—" she said as he backed around and maneuvered the car down the private drive to the main street. "I know we need time alone, but I'm worried about Alain. He's so attached to you, I'm afraid that finding out Natalie was your daughter must have come as a huge shock."

"There's no question he's been deeply affected."

She bit her lip. "He was so quiet at dinner, I wouldn't be surprised if he regretted finding that letter. It's only natural he feels possessive of your attention. My heart aches for him."

"You think mine doesn't?" he bit out before starting the motor. "That's one of the reasons you and I need to talk tonight."

They left the city and climbed the steep hillside past fields of wild narcissi to the little village of Caux. With the windows down, Rachel was able to breathe in their glorious scent. The car negotiated the many corkscrew turns and finally entered another private road.

She'd had an idea Tris was taking her to his house. It turned out to be an exquisite brown and white chalet. The dark green shutters and ornately hand-carved window boxes brimming with flowers were a delight.

He parked in front which gave out on a jaw-dropping view of the lake. The beauty of the fantastic panorama drew a moan from her throat. She'd never seen anything so magnificent.

"On the ship you tried to describe this view to me, but there's no substitute for the real thing. You have to be here to understand." After a short silence, "Where did Bernard and Francoise live?"

"Near my parents. We're keeping the house in the family until Alain's old enough to inherit."

"I bet he goes over there a lot."

"Too often."

She lowered her head. "The poor darling. Both parents gone. I can't imagine it. Losing my dad to a heart attack was hard enough, and I was already twenty-eight.

"Since meeting Alain, I think it would be best if Natalie and I stayed at a hotel this week. He needs to get used to the idea that he has a cousin he must share with you."

Tris's body tautened before his head turned in her direction. "I was watching you through dinner and knew you'd come to that conclusion. But that's exactly what's not going to happen."

She shivered at the finality of those words before he got out of the car and came around her side to help. With his hand cupping her elbow, he walked her across the drive and up the steps to the main floor of the chalet.

Rachel tried not to be affected by his solid body brushing against hers, but it was impossible. Since telling his family how they'd met, she'd been bombarded by memories of the two of them entwined in each other's arms as they'd walked on deck, unaware other people were around.

She was still incredulous they were together again, albeit under vastly different circumstances.

He unlocked the front door and escorted her inside an interior more modern than his parents' home. It exuded its own contemporary style and elegance. However the moment she stepped in the spacious living room, it was the sight of the Alps through the picture windows that caught her attention and held her riveted.

Every day he woke up to this corner of paradise.

Yet after being with him tonight while he'd interacted with Natalie, she had no doubts he would relocate to New Hampshire if necessary to be with his daughter.

Rachel felt his presence behind her and spun around, afraid to get too close to him. Though he had no memory of her, she remembered every breathtaking second of their rapture-filled time aboard ship. Her heart was thudding too hard. His nearness confused her, stirring her senses so she couldn't think clearly.

His hands went to his hips in a wholly male stance. "This is Natalie's rightful home." He broke the tense silence. "She should have been living here all along." His breathing sounded ragged.

"Tell me one thing, Rachel— What in the name of all that's holy stopped you from calling my parents' house to find out why you hadn't heard from me?"

She made the mistake of looking into those fiercely dark depths where once years ago she'd seen desire blazing for her.

Not anymore, she groaned inside. His rage had reached its peak.

"Surely you can understand why."

"No," he came back in a withering tone. "After what we shared on the ship, if you'd been the one who hadn't answered my phone calls or letters, I would have moved heaven and earth to find out why."

"You say that now because you have a daughter and are speaking from hindsight," she cried, "but *I* was there."

His brows furrowed menacingly. "So was I! That photograph is evidence."

She took a step backward, a reaction that only seemed to enflame him more. His mouth had stretched into a thin line.

Rachel shook her head. "But you don't have any memory of that time period. I-it isn't as simple as you want to make it out to be," she faltered. "Our relationship can't be explained away in such a cut and dried manner. The reality is, we only knew each other for nine days," her voice trembled.

"Long enough to make a baby," he thundered.

"Couples get pregnant all the time without the commitment being there."

"I gave you my ring. We were planning to get married!"

Her breathing grew shallow. "I know. But after waiting weeks without hearing from you—not one word or phone call—I had to believe you'd changed your mind. How could I possibly have known you were lying in a coma, unable to contact me?" she almost shouted.

Worse than the stream of French invective pouring from his lips was the wintry look in his eyes.

"Tris—what else could I think except that

once you'd rejoined your hockey friends at training camp, you looked back on our experience as nothing more than a holiday romance?"

He shook his head. "You didn't have the right to decide that on your own. Not after I'd proposed to you and we'd been intimate."

"A lot of guys say things they don't mean in the heat of the moment. We were young, a-and reckless."

His hand went to the back of his neck in a frustrated gesture. "I'm not the kind of man who goes around proposing to every woman I meet."

"I know that now, but twelve years ago you were only nineteen. You saw the picture. We were a bunch of students having a lark. It was perfectly understandable that once you left the ship, you would have lost interest in me and decided to end our relationship the way you did.

"Try to look at it from my point of view. During the crossing I was available and we both had time on our hands. The setting was perfect. We thoroughly enjoyed every minute together. But as time went on without my hearing from you, it was clear to me I was only an interlude in your life. Not your *raison d'etre,*" she said in a tremulous whisper.

Lines marred his handsome features. *"Damn you, Rachel."*

"I damned you my whole pregnancy while I waited to hear from you," she rejoindered, fighting the tears stinging her eyes.

"The agony was so terrible my appetite failed and I started losing weight. Pretty soon I fell behind in my studies. Madame Soulis called my parents. They insisted I come straight home.

"I fought them because I was still hoping you would phone me, or show up at the school, or send me a postcard—any sign to indicate you still wanted me in your life. It never happened!" Her cry reverberated in the room.

"Eventually I flew home. My parents took one look at me and made an appointment for me to see a doctor. When I told him everything, he examined me and discovered I was pregnant."

A grim look of self-recrimination broke out on Tris's face. "Was I so besotted with you, I didn't bother to use protection?"

"No. You were very careful about that. When I told the doctor, he explained that nothing's completely safe."

She heard his sharp intake of breath. "Did we make love more than once?"

His question reminded her how completely surreal their situation was that he had to ask her for every piece of information about the most memorable time of her entire life.

"We slept together the last two nights on the ship, and the next night at a hotel in Geneva where we had dinner. After that you took me to school in a taxi. It was purgatory watching you drive away."

His hooded eyes scrutinized her relentlessly. "Was I your first?"

She looked everywhere except at him. "Yes. I'd dated several guys in high school, but I didn't know the meaning of passion until I met you."

After a palpable silence, "Did I take advantage of you?"

Only an honorable man would have asked her that.

"No, Tris. What we felt for each other was entirely mutual. We tried to control ourselves, but gave up after the second day at sea. When we started to feel the effects of the hurricane, I got frightened and asked you to hold me all night.

"One thing led to another. In all honesty, I was always out of control where you were concerned. I'd fallen in love with you and never wanted to let you go.

"But for the rest of my pregnancy I hated you because you weren't there to share it with me. Then Natalie was born...

"One look at her precious face and I let my

anger go because she was your living image. Our daughter represents the best of both of us. From that day on, I never looked back."

His features hardened. "When she got old enough, what did you tell her about me?"

"That I was just a girl on a ship with whom you had a good time. Once we said goodbye, you promptly forgot me and wouldn't welcome learning there were consequences of our time together."

"She accepted that?"

"Yes! You don't have to be grown up to understand how humiliating it would be to have to beg for love if it isn't freely given."

He paced the floor, then wheeled around. "How did you manage?"

She thought she understood what he was asking.

"My parents helped me. They're saints. Slowly I got my university degree. After Natalie started first grade, I worked part-time at various jobs, but took summers and holidays off to be with her. Last year I bought the townhouse."

"Tell me about Steve."

He leaped topics so fast, she had a hard time keeping up. She hadn't once thought of Steve since leaving Concord. Guilt engulfed her. "He's a wonderful man."

"And?" he prodded.

"We haven't dated long enough yet, but my feelings for him have been growing," she defended. "He's been particularly attentive to Natalie."

"Unfortunately for him he's gone after the wrong woman."

Her heart pounded furiously. "Be careful, Tris. Don't base what you think you know about me on a nine day experience you'll never remember."

He gave a negligent shrug of his shoulders. "I concede you're the keeper of our memories. You're also an attractive thirty-year-old who's still not married. That tells me a lot about you."

The satisfied gleam in his eye could only mean one thing. He thought she'd never gotten over her love affair with him. Needing to disabuse him of that fact she said, "Natalie's happiness has always come ahead of every other consideration."

"Meaning she doesn't like any man who gets too close to you." His mocking smile defeated her. "I have the same problem with Alain who let me know he isn't keen on my receptionist."

So there *was* someone in his life…

"I'm not surprised," Rachel murmured. "The look on his face tonight while he was studying the photograph tore me apart. He's jealous of your attention to Natalie."

"So I noticed."

"It's tragic." Rachel could commiserate with Alain's pain. Over the years she'd suffered enough from jealousy just thinking about Tris with someone else. Of other children who had fathers. It was time to change the subject. Right now she didn't want to be reminded of the list of women who desired a relationship with him.

"After hearing what you told me about our relationship, I'm convinced that if my accident hadn't happened, we'd be married right now and might even have another child or two."

"Don't go there," she said, taking a shallow breath. "We can't rewrite history, Tris."

"Not history—no—but the future. Excuse me while I take this call."

While she'd been talking, his cell phone had rung. He pulled it from his pocket and checked the caller ID before speaking.

"Maman? Qu'est-ce qui se passe?"

Rachel glanced at her watch. It was after 11:00 p.m. Swiss time. No wonder his mother was calling.

"J'arrive a l'instant."

Tris hung up. "I'll go for the kids and be

back shortly. You and Natalie have the run of the next level, so feel free to explore. My staff will have already taken your luggage to your rooms earlier." Before she could think to protest, his long, swift strides carried him away.

She watched out the window for him. He started up the car and headed down the drive. His headlights reflected off the twists and turns of the precarious mountain road descending to the town below. Montreux glittered like a constellation of stars in a far off galaxy.

Rachel felt like she'd entered another dimension. It was almost as if she'd been asleep in a time capsule, and had suddenly awakened to discover everything was different because she'd lost her bearings. Except that Tris was in this new dimension, too.

A Tris who was different, yet in some ways achingly the same.

Smothering a troubled cry, she hurried over to the staircase that took her to the next floor where she and Natalie would be staying. Tris had rejected any talk of her and Natalie moving to a hotel.

Two charming bedrooms with private bathrooms and an adjoining balcony had been prepared for them. Tris had left gift boxes on their beds which were covered with those fabulous

Swiss eiderdown quilts Rachel loved. He'd had flowers placed in their rooms.

Deciding to wait for Natalie so they could open their presents together, she reached for her suitcase and put everything away in drawers and the closet. When that was completed, she went next door and unpacked Natalie's luggage.

While she was hanging up the last of the blouses, her daughter came running in the room. "Mom?"

"I'm right here."

Rachel emerged from the closet and was almost knocked over by Natalie's hug. She lifted shining eyes to her. "Caux is so fantastic! And this chalet! It looks exactly like the pictures in *Heidi*. I love it here so much I can't stand it!

"Just think—if you hadn't decided to come to Switzerland to school, you would never have met Dad. He lives in the most beautiful place in the entire world!"

"I agree," Rachel responded quietly.

"Hey—what's this?" Natalie had picked up the package on top of the quilt.

"It looks like a welcome home present from your father."

"Do you think it's okay if I open it now?"

"I'm sure he'd be disappointed if you didn't."

She carefully undid the wrapping and pulled a tissue packed item from the box. A card fell out with it.

"*Ma belle fille*—when you lift the lid on the chalet, you'll hear the mechanism play the *Sleeping Beauty* waltz. That's how I think of you, Natalie. My little Sleeping Beauty who just woke up to fill her father's heart with joy."

Tears welled in Rachel's throat. When she looked at Natalie, moisture bathed her daughter's cheeks. After removing the paper, they both cried in delight to see a miniature chalet music box that looked exactly like Tris's house.

Natalie lifted the lid and the music of Tchaikovsky filled the room. The sweetest smile broke out on her face. After it stopped playing she said, "I have to find dad!"

Tris couldn't have given her anything she loved more.

Curious to know what was on the other bed, Rachel went to her room and opened the gaily wrapped package. There was an accompanying note.

This would have been yours twelve years ago.

With trembling hands she undid the tissue. Inside was a small music box of the Chateau de Chillon.

A turn of the key and the mechanism played "Variation on the Theme of Paganini."

She bowed her head, remembering that uncomfortable moment at his parents' house when he'd trained accusing eyes on her for keeping all knowledge of his daughter from him. If their positions were reversed, would she be able to find it in her heart to understand his explanation? Forgive him?

Rachel wanted to believe it, yet the music was a bittersweet reminder that even though he'd listened to her reasons just now, she feared it would be too much to hope he would ever truly let go of his anger.

"Thanks for the music box, Dad. I love you so much."

Tris hugged his daughter tightly. "I love you. Get a good sleep."

"You, too. Oh, before I go to bed I have a present for you. It's from my nana. Just a minute and I'll get it." Natalie dashed from the room.

Curious to know what Rachel's mother would have sent to him, he waited impatiently for his daughter who returned in a flash.

"Here—" She handed him a lunch-size sack, tied at the neck with a ribbon.

"What's this?"

"I don't know. She said it was personal, that mom doesn't even know about it. I was supposed to give it to you in private after I got to Switzerland."

"Thank you, *petite*."

"Goodnight, Dad."

"*Bon nuit*. We'll go exploring tomorrow."

"I can't wait!"

As soon as she slipped out the door, he opened the sack. Inside was a wrapped package with a note on the top.

Dear Tris, at the peak of my daughter's pain, she threw these out. I was afraid she might regret it one day, so I gathered them up and kept them without her knowledge. Now I'm glad I did. I understand you suffer from headaches since your memory loss. Maybe these will help. Affectionately, Kathleen Marsden.

He undid the package. Out fell thirty or more glossy snapshots, each one giving him the lost history of his time on the ship and in Geneva with Rachel.

The breath left his lungs. No wonder he'd fallen so hard. With blond hair almost to her waist and those crystalline-green eyes, she was a raving beauty.

There were close-ups of her, of him, all taken against various backdrops. Shots of both of them together with their arms wrapped around each other laughing, hugging, kissing in fun. Kissing in passion…

Mon Dieu. He hardly recognized himself.

Weeks ago he'd told Alain that they'd been young and reckless students who'd gotten carried away in the heat of the moment.

But here was the definitive proof that he and Rachel had been two people wildly in love. He could feel the vibes between them lifting right off the paper.

A groan of pain lodged in his throat. How in the hell could she have thought he'd just been using her? Yet the fact that she'd thrown out these pictures was proof she'd believed it.

Ever since Natalie had opened the door of the townhouse to him, he'd been searching his soul to understand.

He lowered his head, trying to put himself in Rachel's place. That's when he noticed one of the photos had fallen to the floor. He picked it up. There she was, a girl-woman with an alluring combination of innocence and enough love-light in her eyes to blind him.

As he continued to study her, the answer came to him. When he hadn't phoned her, it was the girl part of her who hadn't had the confidence to find out why. But it was the woman who'd gone on with courage to bear their child and raise her to be the most satisfying daughter he could ever have imagined.

Slowly Tris gathered up the photos and put them in his dresser. He owed Rachel's mother a debt of gratitude he could never repay. Soon he would find the right way to thank her.

Unfortunately he had a crisis on his hands that needed to be dealt with tonight. When he'd driven to his parents' to get the kids, his father had informed him that Alain had decided to sleep at their house and had already gone to bed.

Alarmed over this development which wasn't entirely unexpected, Tris drew out his cell phone to call the house. His mother answered.

"Sorry to disturb you, Maman, but I need to speak to Alain. Even if he's asleep, I'd like you to wake him up."

"I'm glad you called. To be honest, I'm worried about him, too. *Un moment.*"

After a minute he heard, "Uncle Tris?" The boy hadn't been asleep or he would have been able to hear it in his voice.

"Hi."

"How come you're calling?"

"Because I miss you around here. How about going fishing with me in the morning?"

There was a silence, then, "Alone?"

"*Oui, mon gars.* Just the two of us. I'll come by for you at six, so set your alarm."

"I'll be ready."

"*Dors bien, Alain.*"

After they'd hung up, he went down to the second floor and knocked on Rachel's door. She didn't answer. Wondering if she and Natalie were together, he stood outside his daughter's room to listen, but was met with silence.

It was vital he talk to Rachel. He tried the handle on her door. It gave. He put his head inside the darkened room and called her name. Still no answer. She wasn't in bed.

Noticing the door to the balcony was open, he stole across the room. From the threshold he could see her robe-clad silhouette standing at the railing. The fragrant night breeze gently disheveled her blond hair, causing it to swish against her shoulders in a seductive motion she wasn't aware of.

Twelve years ago he could imagine the wind off the ocean causing her hair to stream behind her like a pennant. One of the pictures had shown him standing behind her, holding her in his arms. He could feel the silken strands whipping around them while they watched the waves growing more ferocious.

Tris's body quickened as if it had suddenly remembered that moment on deck, even if his mind hadn't.

"Rachel?"

She whirled around, clutching the lapels of her modest toweling robe to her throat. It was an utterly feminine gesture, revealing a surprising vulnerability. "I—I didn't know you were there—"

"Forgive me. I knocked and called out. We need to talk before I go to bed. Do you want me to come back after you're dressed?"

"No—I—I mean, it's all right." She stayed where she was. "Is something wrong with Natalie?"

"Not for the moment. It's Alain I'm worried about."

"So am I," her voice trembled. "Natalie told me he went to bed after we left your parents' house."

"I just got off the phone with him. We're going fishing early in the morning. I expect us to be back by ten, but if we're a little late, I don't want Natalie thinking I've deserted her on her first morning home with me."

Even from the distance he could tell her body had stiffened. "I told you we should have stayed at a hotel during this visit, Tris. Then Natalie wouldn't have expectations, and Alain wouldn't feel supplanted in your affections."

His temper flared. "This is their home. This is where they belong. I thought I'd made that clear to you. Under the circumstances I'll explain to Natalie myself."

"No, wait—" she cried as he turned to leave. "I have an idea." There was an urgency in her tone. It hovered in the air, preventing him from walking out on her.

Still holding on to the door jamb, he drew in a deep breath. "Go on."

"Are you taking a boat out tomorrow?"

"No. We'll hike to a stream and do some fly fishing."

"Where?"

"The Gorge du Chauderon."

He heard her hesitation before she said, "Isn't that near Les Avants?"

"You visited there, too?" he bit out.

"Yes," she answered softly. "Every time the school planned an excursion, I went with them hoping I might bump into you by accident…or better yet, that you would see me and we could talk about what went wrong."

He cursed under his breath. How long would it take before he stopped reacting to the fact that she'd been so close during those two months in Geneva while he suffered a permanent blackout of memory?

He raked a hand through his hair. "What was your idea?"

"I thought Natalie and I could bring the car and meet you for lunch. If you're late, it won't matter because we'll play tourist. I seem to remember a charming little café in the town center."

"Les Deux Couronnes."

"I'm sure that was the name. Is it still there?"

"Yes," he muttered.

"Then we'll look for you around eleven. Please show up by eleven-thirty at the latest, otherwise your daughter will insist we send out a search party for you, creating a national incident. In case you didn't realize it yet, she's absolutely crazy about her father."

Her comment, infused with a hint of levity, caught him off guard. "I'll keep that in mind." He fished in his pocket for his keys. "On my way out, I'll leave the Mercedes key on your dresser. The car's got plenty of gas."

"You trust me to drive it?" She was definitely teasing him now.

He shifted his weight. "When I see the magnificent job you've done raising our daughter, I dare say I trust you with my life. So why not my car which is easily replaced?"

"I'll try not to do that much damage."

In spite of certain emotions churning him up inside, his lips twitched. "I'm relieved to hear it. *Bon nuit, Rachel.*"

"Goodnight."

As he started to leave, she called to him again. "Thank you for everything you've done for us, Tris. Between you and your parents, your generosity is so overwhelming, I don't know how I'll ever be able to repay you."

He looked back over his shoulder at her. "You still don't get it, do you. But one day soon you will."

CHAPTER SIX

BY THE time Rachel and Natalie had finished their shopping, a mixture of locals and tourists had started filling the tables of the Deux Couronnes. Luckily she'd been able to secure a spot out on the *terrasse* where they could watch for Tris and Alain.

A waiter approached. *"Vous desirez, madame?"*

"Deux Grapillons, s'il vous plait."

"Bien."

After he walked away, Natalie looked up from the postcards she was writing to her friends. "Your French sounded pretty good, Mom. I want to speak French like Dad."

"Under your father's tutelage, you will."

"What did you order us?"

"Grape juice. It's—"

"I know," Natalie broke in. "It's what you used to drink. I bet you're excited to be here."

"Yes."

"Then how come you're so quiet?"

Rachel might have known Natalie would pick up on any change in her mood. Last night Tris's parting remark had filled her with fresh anxiety. She hadn't been able to fall asleep for a long time.

"I'm concerned about Alain."

"He misses his parents, huh."

"It's more than that." There was no easy way to say it, but Rachel had to make Natalie understand the depth of Alain's pain.

Once their drinks had arrived she said, "Alain has loved his uncle since he was born. Now that he no longer has parents, he looks at Tris as his father. They've lived together for a whole year. Do you understand what I'm trying to tell you?"

"Not exactly."

"Alain's afraid."

"Of what?" Natalie took an experimental sip. "Um. This is pretty good, but it needs ice."

"Most places in Europe don't serve ice. You have to learn to enjoy drinks without it."

"How come?"

Rachel let out a sigh of frustration. "Honey— I'm trying to tell you something important."

"You mean about Alain."

"Yes. Now that your father has discovered he has you, Alain's worried Tris won't love him anymore."

"Why?"

A simple question deserving a simple answer, but there wasn't one.

"Because you're his daughter, and Tris is only his nephew. He thinks his uncle will start favoring you and forget him."

"Dad wouldn't do that!"

Total loyalty already. It was astounding. What Rachel found even more amazing was that Natalie exhibited no jealousy of her cousin. She'd always wanted a brother or sister.

"We both know your father loves you equally, but Alain doesn't." After a pause, "What do you suppose we could do to help him not be so upset?"

Natalie frowned. "I don't know. Be his friend?"

Rachel could feel her eyes smarting. "That's a wonderful sugges—"

"There they are!" Natalie had seen them across the street at the same time as Rachel. She jumped up excitedly from her chair. "I'll show them where we parked so they can put their fishing poles away. Can I have the key to dad's car?"

With that fluttery sense of anticipation every time Tris came near, Rachel reached for her purse and handed Natalie the key.

"Thanks." She dashed off.

More people had congregated outside the café, but Tris's handsome features and tall physique stood out in the crowd. He looked attractive in anything, but never more so than in the well-worn, thigh-molding jeans and T-shirt he was wearing.

A too familiar ache passed through her body—the resonant sign that the fire on her part had never been completely extinguished. To fan it now might create an inferno that would devour her. She wasn't sure it was wise to stay in Switzerland much longer.

In a few more days Natalie would feel so at home here, Rachel could leave for Concord and let her daughter enjoy the time alone with her father until school started. After that, they could work out a reasonable visitation schedule that would be best for everyone concerned, especially Alain.

Natalie could come again at Thanksgiving and Christmas. Looking ahead to next year, she could fly over and stay for spring break. Much as Rachel despised the thought of visitation, it was the only solution. Hundreds of thousands of families in the world managed to deal with it.

Tris didn't really want to build a hotel in New Hampshire, let alone live there. His life was here. He had a receptionist he was interested in, otherwise he wouldn't have brought up the other woman in conversation.

The thing he should do was bring Alain to Concord with him on the odd weekend. Somehow it would all work out. It *had* to.

With that decision made, Rachel summoned the waiter and ordered sandwiches and fries. In a few minutes the kids and Tris joined her. There were other dark haired males in the café, but only one turned every feminine head as he made his way through the lunch crowd.

Rachel purposely greeted Alain without looking at Tris. "Did you catch any trout?"

"No," he said glumly before sitting down in the chair on her left. "Uncle Tris thinks they'll start biting later in the day when there are more insects out."

What she didn't hear Alain say was that he wished more than anything he and his uncle could have fished all day. The thought gave Rachel an idea.

"I haven't been fishing in years. Maybe after lunch we could go back to your favorite spot and see if we can catch enough for dinner." She turned to her daughter. "What do you say, Natalie?"

"That would be fun." She sounded like she meant it. Whether it was because of their prior conversation, or the fact that she was open to any suggestion because she was with her father, Rachel was thankful for Natalie's positive response.

"Good. Then let's do it." Turning her head for Alain's approval, she accidentally ran into Tris's veiled gaze.

"Maybe tomorrow," he murmured.

Right now Tris didn't seem to be looking at her as friend or foe, rather something in between. It was a subtle improvement from his initial rage. If only it would last until she left Switzerland...

The *garcon* appeared at that moment to serve them. *"Bon appetit."*

Natalie stared at her plate, then at Rachel. "What is it?"

"A *croque-monsieur*," Tris informed her.

Their daughter tried to repeat the words, but made a hash of it.

Both Rachel and Tris chuckled. Their eyes met again. This time her heart turned over. Just then she was back on the ship enjoying one of the many private moments with him that had caused her to fall so deeply in love.

"What's in it, Dad?"

"Ham and cheese," her father murmured, still looking at Rachel.

"Hey, they have French fries here." Natalie ate one. "Um. They're good."

"They should be, honey. The Swiss invented them."

Her brown eyes widened. "Honest?"

"Ask your father if you don't believe me. He's the one who told me."

Tris's mouth broke into an engaging smile, stealing all the air from her lungs. "I'm almost afraid to find out what other unsubstantiated facts I told you in order to impress you while we were on the ship."

"You'd be surprised."

Again she had the sensation of déjà vu.

On their first day at sea he'd continually flirted with her. He'd made up some of the most outrageous statements just to make her laugh. Something would flicker in the recesses of his dark eyes, the way it was happening now—exciting her, thrilling her until she didn't know where to go with all her emotions.

"I don't want a sandwich. Can I order pizza?"

Alain's question shattered the moment, reminding Rachel she wasn't alone with Tris.

"Pizza?" Natalie sounded shocked.

"It's not exactly like ours, honey."

"Since we have another place to be in a little while, Alain, we'd better eat what Rachel ordered so we won't be late." Tris tucked into his food with obvious relish.

"Where are we going, Dad?"

"That's for me to know, and you to find out," he teased.

Natalie giggled, but Alain only toyed with his meal. Clearly he was upset at not being able to manipulate the situation. Rachel understood the reason behind his behavior, but she admired the gentle yet firm way Tris handled his nephew by not giving in to him on every issue. How else would the boy learn to cope?

Within fifteen minutes they left the café and walked around the corner to the car. Tris was behaving very mysteriously. Rachel had to admit she was as curious as Natalie about their destination.

Natalie climbed in the back seat with Rachel. It left Alain to get in front with his uncle, thereby averting a minor crisis. She reached for her hand and gave it a squeeze. Natalie squeezed back.

Rachel had never loved this kindhearted daughter of hers more than right now. Judging by the look in Tris's eyes as he glanced at the two of them through the rearview mirror, he was aware of Natalie's unselfish gesture, too.

The trip through the mountains was one of enchantment. Rachel felt as if she were seeing the bucolic Swiss countryside for the first time. Twelve years ago there'd been too much pain. That wasn't the case today. Being with Tris had made her euphoric, the most dangerous state of mind for her.

They drove through several Alpine villages including Gruyeres where the world famous cheese was made. When Natalie asked if they were going to stop, Tris informed her they would come another day.

"Right now I'm craving dessert. I thought we'd get some further on in Broc."

"Broc? You're in for the treat of your life," Rachel couldn't help commenting.

Natalie's head jerked around. "You know where Dad's taking us?"

"I do now. You'll think you died and went to heaven." Again Rachel's eyes encountered Tris's gaze through the mirror. She recognized his excitement. On the ship he'd told her about this place. Now he was eager to show Natalie his world.

If only Rachel could have found the courage to contact Tris's family in the beginning…

But it hadn't happened.

Somehow she had to stop allowing herself to be riddled by regrets and what if's. The important thing here was to be thankful that Natalie and her father had found each other. Tris would be there to help guide her through the ups and downs of her teenage years when a girl needed her father so badly.

Rachel's eyes strayed to Alain. The poor thing. Opening that letter had been like letting the genie out of the bottle. She wished she could put her arms around him, not only to thank him, but to comfort him. He'd lost his parents at the same age Natalie was now.

The dynamics of the situation were incredibly precarious. Before there could be any kind of satisfactory resolution, Rachel had a premonition things would grow a lot more difficult for everyone involved.

"How can we have dessert here?"

Natalie's voice brought Rachel back to her surroundings. Tris had pulled up in front of a sprawling old building. He shut off the motor.

"Step outside the car, *petite,* and you'll figure it out."

She undid her seat belt and scrambled from the back seat. Tris came around to help. Rachel's body went hot as his gaze made a thorough inventory of her face and figure. It was exactly the way he used to look at her when she would open her cabin door to him, be it morning or night.

"Oh my gosh—I can smell chocolate!"

"That's the aroma of the cocoa beans roasting," Tris said though he was still staring at Rachel. "This is where they manufacture chocolate bars. You're going to see the process from start to finish."

A squealing sound came out of Natalie, but her cousin made no move to join them.

"Come on, Alain." Tris opened the front passenger door.

"I've been here before. I'll wait for you in the car."

Rachel couldn't bear it that he was hurting. "You know what, Alain? I've had the tour, too."

She turned to Tris, imploring him with her eyes to understand. "Give me the keys. We'll drive into the village and walk around until you and Natalie are through. As I recall, the tour takes about an hour."

There was no point in everyone being miserable. Tris needed time alone with his daughter. This was the perfect opportunity.

Rachel could sense his hesitation. She held her breath before he finally handed her the keys.

"I'll try not to get lost," she said in a dead-pan face.

Under other circumstances she might have gotten an amused smile from him.

"Have fun," she called to Natalie, then went around to the driver's seat and got behind the wheel.

Once she started the car and they'd driven out to the main road, she looked over at Alain.

"After we get you a pizza, let's find a tackle shop. When Tris and I were on the ship, he told me how much he loved your father. It was Bernard this and Bernard that. Among other things I found out your dad was the expert fly fisher-man in the family.

"Why don't we buy some hand-tied flies that are guaranteed to work in the gorge? Your uncle said we could go fishing tomorrow. It'll be fun to surprise him by catching lots of fish, don't you think?"

He slanted her a contemplative glance. "I guess."

At least it wasn't a flat no. If her prayers were answered, Alain would have success tomorrow. The praise from Tris would do him a world of good. Holding only the best thoughts, she headed for the center of the village.

They came to a tiny café and ordered two individual pizzas to go. The *serveuse* behind the counter told them where to find the sporting goods store. Rachel was still full from her sandwich, but she started to eat her pizza anyway. Soon Alain copied her. They ate as they walked along the quaint street.

She was glad to see his appetite had improved. By the time they'd entered the shop, he'd finished his off.

"My French isn't up to telling the man what we want. You'll have to do it."

Alain nodded and approached him.

While the two of them got into a discussion, Rachel found a waste basket and deposited the other half of her pizza. Then she joined them at the rear of the store. The flies were visible in containers beneath the counter. She pulled out her packet of travelers cheques and signed one to pay for everything.

With their transaction completed, they headed for the car. She opened the trunk. Before Alain put the flies away in his tackle box, she asked him to show her what he'd bought.

He'd purchased a half dozen flies with brown and white bodies streaked by a red line. "The man told me most trout don't see a lot of flies in the brushiest part of the gorge. But he said if

I swing one of these streamers into the pools behind the rocks, I'll catch some."

"I guess if I were a fish, these would look yummy."

Alain gave her an extra long glance before hiding the sack. Then they retraced the route to the chocolate factory on the outskirts of the village. For the moment he was tolerating her presence, but no one knew how long it would last.

While Tris was talking to Guy, he heard footsteps behind him. He looked around, hoping it was Rachel. After today's incident at the factory, she needed to be told that Alain was Tris's problem. He would deal with that situation from here on out.

As if thinking about him conjured him up, his nephew had appeared in the kitchen wearing his pajamas.

Tris told Guy he would have to call him later, and hung up.

"Looks like you're ready for bed." At least Alain hadn't asked to go back to his grandparents to sleep.

"Can we leave to go fishing at the same time in the morning?"

Fishing? Tris had all but forgotten about it,

but it was obvious Alain had been counting on it. "Of course. I'll let Rachel and Natalie know so they'll be ready."

"Do they have to come?"

Tris rubbed his jaw in frustration. "As I recall, it was Rachel's idea because she knew how disappointed you were to cut things short today."

His nephew lowered his eyes and turned to leave, but Tris wouldn't let him go without giving him a hug. "See you down here at six. I love you."

Alain ran off without saying the same thing back. It was a first for him.

Tris stood there in a quandary. These were early days. In time Alain would learn to accept Natalie and adjust to the situation. But the niggling thought continued to torture him that Alain might not adjust. Couldn't.

Unwilling to let things deteriorate any further, Tris decided to go after him. He'd almost reached the door, when Rachel unexpectedly entered the kitchen. She was still dressed in the leaf green top and white pants she'd worn earlier. It was difficult to keep his eyes from straying over the curving mold of her body.

"Here." She handed him what looked like a yogurt carton with tiny holes in the top.

"What's this?"

"Put it in the microwave for thirty seconds and you'll find out."

She'd mimicked what he'd said to Natalie earlier in the day. Intrigued, he did her bidding. At fifteen seconds he could smell chocolate. He shot her a questioning glance, feeling a strong pull on his senses that had nothing to do with food.

"When Alain and I got back to the factory, you were still on the tour. I asked the woman in reception if she would do me a favor. It's my gift to you for making our daughter so happy."

He opened the carton. Melted dark chocolate. His favorite kind.

"On the ship you told me how good it was fresh from the vat."

"Let's test it and find out, shall we?" He put his index finger into the warm, delicious looking goo and held it up to her mouth. "You first."

As he watched her take a hesitant, dainty bite with her lips, his heart hammered against his ribs. He'd kissed those enticing lips before. Many, many times, with her full permission. The proof lay in the pictures tucked away in his drawer, but he had no memory of the experience.

"I think it's time to make one," he muttered indistinctly.

"W-what did you say?"

For an answer, he pressed his lips to her chocolate covered mouth, needing to taste what had been offered so provocatively without her realizing it.

Driven by a need that had been growing since he'd first laid eyes on her at the townhouse, he trapped her against the counter and started to deepen their kiss.

"No, Tris—" She pushed him away and spun around to turn on the tap. She needed to clean the chocolate off her mouth.

While Tris waited for his breathing to return to normal, he watched her wash any residue chocolate off her face. Rachel could deny it all she wanted, but for that infinitesimal second before she'd cried out, he'd felt her respond. It ignited sensations inside him he feared weren't going to go away.

He put the carton on the counter. "If I hadn't had that accident, this is exactly what we would have ended up doing. Thank you for the gift. You and I now share one living memory from the past."

She clung to the sink without looking at him. "I hope that's the last of the surprises. Natalie or Alain could have walked in just now."

The mention of his nephew had the effect of cooling his ardor.

"I'm sorry he was difficult today."

"It's not your fault. It's not anyone's fault." Her voice shook. She finally turned around to face him. "But he's in pain."

"I agree. Still—at this point we need to lay some ground rules. Natalie's never going to go away. The sooner he faces that fact, the better off he'll be. I need your cooperation."

Her face closed up. "I refuse to apologize for trying to make him feel better today. One look in his eyes and—"

"I'm not asking for an apology, Rachel. Your kindness to him was a revelation. But if you interfere, I can't discipline him no matter how well intentioned."

"I'm the intruder here."

"Wrong," he fired back. "I brought you and Natalie home to stay. It's a *fait accompli*. What I need is your promise that from now on you'll respond the way you would if he were my son. In other words, let me handle him."

"I'll try, but that'll be difficult to do."

"Nothing's going to change the situation except time."

"What if nothing changes?" she blurted. Her question echoed his fears.

"It will," he said with more certainty than he felt. "Natalie will win him over. I'm just thankful we have a sensitive daughter whose ability to love everyone is rare. I've been around you long enough to realize the credit goes to you for cultivating those strengths."

"No, Tris. She came that way. Alain has that same sweetness. I could tell it over the phone when he first called me. His only concern was to help you overcome your headaches. It's obvious he worships you to the point he doesn't want anything to happen to you."

"Alain worries too much."

She studied him pensively. "After your accident, was the surgery extensive?"

"No. The only thing the doctor could do was relieve pressure on the brain. The rest was up to my body to restore itself."

"What a terrible experience you had to go through." Her voice trembled.

"I don't remember any of it. When I woke up, I was able to go home and get on with my life."

"Except that you still get headaches."

"Occasionally."

"I bet it's more than that or Alain would never have been prompted to call me. Tell me the truth. How often do they come?"

"Since I left the hospital, there's been no pattern. Sometimes they hit in clusters. Sometimes I can go several months without one."

"Sounds like migraine."

"Migraine medication doesn't work on me."

"What do you do for them?"

"Sleep them off with an ice bag." His eyes narrowed as he studied her. "Why the sudden concern?"

"Natalie needs to understand so she'll know what to do for you when one comes on. I'm not always going to be around."

"That sounded cryptic," he bit out. "What in the hell are you trying to tell me?"

Her head reared. "What do you mean?"

"Are you trying to say you won't always be here? Do you have a medical condition our daughter isn't aware of?"

"No. Of course not! I only meant that when I go back to Concord, I want her to be reassured that you'll be all right should she discover you're in pain."

His dark brows knit together. "Who said anything about you going anywhere?"

"I live there."

"You're on vacation."

"I—I've been thinking about that." Her voice sounded unsteady. "Since we know Natalie already adores it here, I'll stay another day, then leave. She can stay with you until school starts. That's what you want, isn't it?"

"We've been over this ground before. But what's the rush? I told you Steve is welcome here anytime."

"This isn't about Steve. Can't you see that if I'm not around, Alain won't feel so threatened? I have to go, Tris. Otherwise the situation doesn't have a prayer of working!"

Before he could stop her she'd disappeared from the kitchen. Her abrupt departure touched off his own deep seated worry over his nephew's depressed state of mind.

But to his chagrin, her determination to leave Switzerland had set off other concerns. Ones he didn't dare investigate too closely since they had little to do with either of the children.

CHAPTER SEVEN

"DAD? I just had a bite!"

"Hold on, *petite*. Play with it for a minute, but let it know you're in charge."

"Okay, but it's tugging hard."

"Stay with it. I'm coming."

No no no.

Rachel bowed her head. It wasn't supposed to happen this way. Alain should be the one calling out to his uncle in exhilaration.

They'd been fishing in the gorge all day minus the time taken off for a picnic lunch and snacks provided by Simone, Tris's housekeeper. The longer they went without anyone catching a fish, the more determined Alain was to stick to it.

Natalie was having the time of her life with her father. She couldn't care less how long they stayed out. He was her captive audience.

She chatted about her cat Boots who'd died

of liver disease. Tris heard all about the funeral they'd held. Her grandpa had officiated. She rattled on about her nana, her friends, her favorite movies and music, what she liked and disliked about school, her tonsillectomy.

Further upstream Alain stayed hunkered down by some rocks. He'd been there hours waiting patiently for a brown trout to rise out of the pool and take his brand-new fly.

Why did it have to be Natalie with beginner's luck this late in the day?

"Trust *ma belle fille* to catch the only fish!" Tris called out. "It's big enough for everyone to have part of it for dinner." Pride in his daughter rang in his voice.

Rachel wanted to stay and help Alain, but she was a novice herself. Besides, after Tris's talk with her last night, he wouldn't appreciate her ignoring his wishes to let him handle Alain.

She left her spot to join them. Tris looked surprised that his nephew hadn't come with her. "You two go on." He handed Rachel the keys. "Alain and I will catch up to you at the car."

With a nod to Tris, she and Natalie started down the ravine. After they'd gone a ways, she gave her daughter a hug. "Congratulations."

"I couldn't believe I caught one. I told dad I'd like to come back here again tomorrow."

Her comment gave Rachel the opening she was looking for. "I think that's a terrific idea." Maybe Alain would get lucky.

"Did you have fun?"

"I had a great time."

"I'm sorry you didn't catch one."

"I'm not." They kept on going, picking their way around the rocks and underbrush. "Honey? Now that you're settled here, would you mind very much if I flew back to Concord?"

Natalie looked up at her in surprise. "When?"

"Maybe tomorrow or the next day."

After a silence, "Did Steve ask you to come home?"

"That's not what's important. I've been watching you and your father. He loves you very much. While it's still summer and he's on vacation, I think it's important for the two of you to be alone for a while. Up until now I've had you all to myself."

"Have you told Dad?"

"Yes. We talked about it last night." At least *she'd* talked about it, then hurried off without hearing his response.

"When will you come back?"

"Why don't we leave it open? How about until we miss each other too much."

They reached the car and put their fishing poles away. "Are you going to miss me?"

"Natalie—what a question!" She crushed her in her arms. "You're my whole life, honey."

"I know. I'm going to miss you, too."

But not enough to tell me not to go. That was because Tris had already made their daughter feel safe.

In a few minutes he returned with a taciturn Alain and they headed back to Caux. En route Tris announced he would fix dinner provided everyone helped. Natalie was all for that.

Once they arrived at the house, he divied up the jobs, but Alain was patently unhappy about it. When they sat down to eat, he refused his portion of trout.

Rachel caught Tris's worried glance and decided this was the best time to make her plans known. She put her fork down.

"Tris? I've been talking to Natalie and have made up my mind to leave for New Hampshire in the morning. There are several flights I can take from Geneva, but if you insist on sending me back on your jet, I won't say no." She chuckled.

It was a given he wouldn't let her travel on a commercial flight, so it was best to just cave in ahead of time to avoid argument.

Alain sat straighter in his chair. "You didn't stay very long."

Clearly he sounded pleased by the news. Her instincts had been right. He wanted her gone. But she shivered at the fierceness of Tris's regard trained on her.

Avoiding his eyes she said, "I only planned to come for a few days, Alain. I've a job to get back to."

"Mom's got a boyfriend," Natalie informed him.

Rachel's talk with her daughter about Alain's fear had obviously sunk in. Natalie had purposely introduced Steve into the conversation because she was trying to include Alain by confiding in him. At Natalie's age you told secrets when you wanted to make friends with someone. What a terrific daughter she was.

Alain glanced at Natalie. "What's his name?"

"Steve Clarkson. He's pretty nice," she added. "He came to my last hockey game."

"You play ice hockey?" Alain looked stunned.

"Yup. Do you?"

"No. Uncle Tris won't let me."

"That's a little harsh isn't it, *mon gars?*" Tris interjected. "Because of my head injury, the doctors told me I had to give up hockey after I came out of my coma. Your parents saw what happened to me and made the decision that they would never allow you to play it. One near fatal hockey accident in the Monbrisson family closed that door forever."

Alain's cheeks went a ruddy color. "Natalie's a Monbrisson, and *she* plays."

"She's not your parents' daughter."

The boy fought tears. It killed Rachel to see him this way.

"I know how much you'd like to take it up, Alain. But I'm only carrying out what Bernard and Francoise wanted. Would you expect me to go against their wishes?"

"I wish I'd died with them."

On that horrifying note Alain dashed out of the kitchen. A grim-faced Tris pushed himself away from the table and went after him.

Natalie started to cry. "I didn't know he couldn't play hockey."

"Of course you didn't." Rachel squeezed her arm.

"Mom? I think Alain hates me."

"No he doesn't."

"Maybe I should go home with you."

Rachel moaned. For her daughter to say that, she was hurting for Alain so much it appeared she was ready to sacrifice her own happiness. This was turning into a nightmare.

For once Rachel didn't know how to answer her. "We'll talk about it later. It's getting late. Let's do the dishes."

"Okay," Natalie said in a mournful tone.

They worked together in silence before Natalie dashed up the stairs to shower. After she got in her pajamas, Rachel sat on the side of the bed to talk to her.

"Alain obviously needs more time to get used to you. Just remember that your father loves you desperately. I don't think he could bear it if you left him now."

"I don't want to leave him." Her lower lip trembled. "Maybe you shouldn't go home yet, Mom."

"No one's going anywhere."

Tris had come in the bedroom. He shot Rachel a forbidding glance, defying her to say anything. "Given time, everything's going to be all right, *petite.*"

His gaze swerved to Natalie. The look in his eyes grew tender. "Alain didn't mean what he said. One day soon he's going to be happy again, so forget about what happened at the table. How about a kiss goodnight? We've got another big fishing day tomorrow."

Natalie smiled in relief and threw her arms around his neck.

Rachel could tell there was more Tris had to say to their daughter. She left the room only to discover Alain waiting for her in her own bedroom. He was still dressed in the pants and shirt he'd worn fishing.

"Hi," she said quietly.

His lips pressed together in greeting before he said, "I'm sorry for what happened at dinner."

Tris had to be the one responsible for this apology. Not wanting to undermine him, she sank down on the end of the bed, struggling to find the right words.

"My father died two years ago. I know how hard it is to lose a parent. But Natalie and I realize it was twice as hard for you. There must be times when you can't bear the pain."

She thought he nodded.

"Do you know you're a lot like your uncle?"

Alain looked at her with a puzzled expression.

Rachel smiled kindly at him. "You both want to make the other person happy. That's why you called me in the first place, because you hoped if I told him about the past, his headaches would go away.

"He, in turn, is trying to be the best father to you so *your* pain will go away."

His sober expression didn't change. "Uncle Tris is Natalie's father."

"He wants to be yours, too, but he's afraid he'll never be as wonderful a parent as your father was to you."

The boy eyed her suspiciously. "Did he tell you that?"

"Yes." In a manner of speaking. "When he came to see me and Natalie in Concord, the first thing he told us was how much he loved you. When he told Natalie he wanted her to come to Switzerland, he distinctly said, 'I want you to live with me and Alain.'"

His face fell. "He had to say that. It doesn't mean anything."

"Then how come you haven't been living with your grandparents since the funeral? From what I can tell, they love you to pieces."

A full minute must have passed while he dug the toe of his boot into the floor. "I don't know," he said at long last.

"Maybe you should ask them."

He stuck around for another few seconds. Then, "Maybe I will." In the next instant he was out the door like a shot.

She got up to shower and get ready for bed. The more she thought about it, the more she admired Tris for taking on the responsibility of a twelve-year-old boy. Nephew or not, few single men were that unselfish with their time.

For someone like Tris who ran such a huge business enterprise, it would have been natural to let his parents take over Alain's care. He truly was a remarkable human being. She'd thought so when she'd first met him.

Even at nineteen he'd seemed a breed apart from other guys. Looking back to that time on the ship, he'd been protective as well as loving.

But when she never heard from him again, she began to doubt her own judgment in men. It was the reason why she'd been suspicious of any man who'd tried to get close to her since then.

Who would have dreamed an older Tris would be back in her life, exhibiting the nobility she'd sensed in the younger man? A lesser person might have changed his mind about parenting Alain in order to win over his new-found daughter.

Not Tris. He claimed both children without hesitation. How she loved him for it!

No no no. Not loved. She couldn't be falling in love with him again. *She just couldn't!*

Haunted by the prospect, she climbed under the covers determined to go home and start over with Steve. He'd been trying hard to break through her defenses. It was past time to let him.

Tomorrow she would go fishing with Natalie. If everything didn't fall apart, she would leave for Concord the next day. After setting her alarm, she lay back down willing sleep to come.

To her surprise, she was awakened the next morning by a knock on her door. It couldn't be Natalie. Her daughter would just have walked in. Maybe it was Alain.

Rachel sat up in bed. "Come in."

Her heart thudded when she saw Tris in the aperture dressed casually for their outing. She drew the covers to her chin. "Am I holding everyone up?"

"Have you seen Alain?" He answered her question with a question. His voice sounded several decibels lower than usual.

She smoothed the hair out of her face, sensing his tension. "Not since last night."

"You mean at dinner?"

"No. It was later while you were saying good-night to Natalie. I came in here to get ready for bed and discovered him waiting for me. He wanted to apologize."

"I'm surprised he followed through," Tris said in a grave tone. "I went to his room a minute ago to get him up, but he wasn't there. Neither Simone or Natalie has seen him this morning. If he didn't come in here, then it means he took off and could be anywhere just to thwart me."

"Surely not to thwart you," Rachel rushed to assure him. Pained by the agony in his voice she said, "I think he might have left early to go see his grandparents."

He moved closer to the bed. "What do you know that I don't?"

Without preamble she told him the essence of her conversation with Alain. "He said maybe he would go talk to them."

Tris pulled out his cell phone to call his parents. After a brief discussion he hung up. His features had taken on a chiseled cast.

"What is it?"

"He hasn't been there."

"Then he's probably on his way. He couldn't have been gone long."

"Unless he left here last night after talking to you."

Grasping at any possibility that would comfort him she said, "I doubt that. He probably took off for a friend's house this morning. Does he ride a bike?"

"All the time. But I checked in the lower storage room we use to keep our outdoor equipment. It's still there," he muttered before making several calls. After a half dozen brief exchanges he clicked off. She could tell by his somber look no one had seen Alain.

A shudder rocked her body. "Let's go look for him. Give me a minute to get dressed. Natalie and I will come with you. Is she ready?"

"Yes. Right now she's downstairs eating breakfast. We'll meet you at the car."

The second he left the room she discarded her nightgown and threw on some jeans and a navy cotton top. There was little time to spend on her hair. She brushed it before tying it back with a matching scarf. After stepping into leather sandals, she turned off the alarm which was about to ring and left the room.

When she stepped outside the chalet to join them, an overcast sky greeted her vision. Clouds obscured the mountains across the lake. She felt more humidity in the air and thought they might be in for a light rain later in the day. Nothing as heavy as the weight dragging down her heart.

Tris helped her get in the back of the car. Natalie leaned over the seat to kiss her.

"We'll find him," Rachel answered the question in her daughter's eyes.

Natalie looked at her father. "I bet he's at Grand-mere Louise's by now."

He patted her arm. "You're probably right."

Except Rachel hadn't heard his cell phone ring which meant his parents hadn't found their grandson yet. She scanned the landscape in the hope she might see him.

When they arrived at the house in Montreux, Louise was already in the courtyard waiting for them. They got out of the car to greet her. Natalie reached her first and hugged her.

"I take it there's been no sign of him, Maman."

She shook her head. "Marcel went down to the boathouse to see if he was there. But he just phoned to tell me the boat's still tied up. Right now he's searching for him along the shore."

A gaunt look overlay Tris's striking features. "Then I'll drive around to some of his favorite haunts."

Rachel could hardly bear to see him this upset. "I'll go with you." She turned to Louise. "Could Natalie stay with you?"

"I was just going to suggest it. While we make cookies, we'll put our heads together to figure out where he might be."

Natalie nodded. "See you later, Mom." She gave her and Tris a kiss before going in the house with her grandmother.

Once back in the car Rachel said, "Maybe he went by his old house."

"You're reading my mind. We'll go there first. Another family is leasing it, but they let him in if he asks."

"Does he do it often?"

"In the beginning. However I don't believe he's been there in the last couple of months."

He drove the car along the *Quai des Fleurs* where a lot of private villas, including his deceased brother's, lined the lake. The drive bordered a flowered, palm-lined promenade with benches for people to take in the majesty of the lake and mountains.

If things had worked out differently, Montreux would have become Rachel's home. She would have been the aunt Alain turned to when his world was destroyed. Instead he'd run away from her because she and Natalie were strangers who presented a new threat to his happiness with Tris.

She waited in the car while he went to the door of the Italianate-styled villa to make inquiries. Beyond the ornamental almond and bay trees, heavy foliage covered the grounds of the estate. It would have represented paradise to any child, particularly one as adventurous as Alain.

"No one including the gardener has seen him," he said after getting back inside. "They'll keep an eye out and call me if he should show up." He hit his fist against the steering wheel. "Where would he go? None of his friends have seen him."

She bit her lip. "Could he have gone to your office to talk to your assistant? I don't remember his name."

Tris's head swiveled around in stunned surprise. His dark eyes enveloped her. "You mean Guy? I would never have thought of him."

"I only bring him up because it's apparent Alain regrets ever discovering the letter I wrote you. Since he asked Guy to help him get my parents' phone number, I was thinking Alain might have turned to him."

Tris sucked in his breath. "I pray to God you're right." In the next instant he was on the phone to the man who kept the Monbrisson empire running smoothly while Tris was on vacation.

Rachel could only follow small portions of the French conversation. As they talked she found her mind dwelling on Alain's parents who'd once lived here. It was such a terrible tragedy to happen to a family.

Tris eventually clicked off, bringing her back to the present. When she looked at him, he shook his head. "Nothing. But Guy will alert everyone concerned to be on the lookout for him."

Alain had to be somewhere, her heart cried. "When I miss my father, I go to his grave to feel closer to him. Where's your brother buried?"

Again it seemed she'd surprised him. "The Montreux-Clarens communal cemetery. Alain could have taken the bus there. It's worth investigating."

He started up the engine and they drove away from the estate. Tris followed the signs to Vevey, a nearby town. Before they reached it, they came to the beautifully manicured resting spot dotted with markers and tombs. He pulled to a stop beneath a huge chestnut tree.

"Their headstone is right over there. The tall white one."

Rachel's eyes picked out the gleaming monument at once. Except for an old man walking with a cane, she didn't see another soul. If Alain had already been here, there was no way to tell.

Compelled by the need to pay her respects, Rachel got out of the car and walked toward it. She studied the epitaph.

Bernard and Francoise—In Loving Memory

Tris caught up to her. She glanced at him. The grief she saw written on his unforgettable face prompted her to comfort him. Without conscious thought she reached for his hand.

He gripped hers so hard, he couldn't possibly have known his own strength. She didn't mind. He could crush it if he wanted to, anything to help alleviate his pain. But Rachel recognized the only way to do that was to find Alain.

"Tris? What did Alain enjoy doing the most with his parents?"

"Besides skiing in winter, probably hiking to a favorite spot to camp and fish."

"Where would that be?"

His chest heaved. "There's a forest about an hour's hike from the chalet. The three of them would erect a tent by the stream and cook out."

"When you checked the equipment room this morning, did you notice if any camping gear was missing?"

She heard a rush of air escape his lungs. "Alain keeps his pack and bedroll in his own closet. We'll go back to the house and check."

He started for the car, seemingly unaware he was still gripping her hand. Rachel understood the fear driving him. She had to run to keep up with his long strides.

Once he'd helped her in the car, they retraced the route to Caux in record time. As they entered the foyer of the chalet, Simone appeared. Her anxious expression dealt them another blow, making any questions about Alain's whereabouts unnecessary.

Tris took the stairs three at a time. Rachel trailed him to Alain's bedroom. He opened the door of the walk-in closet.

"His gear's missing."

Encouraged by that announcement, she turned to go to her room and change into clothes more suited for hiking. But when she caught sight of a familiar, well-worn green backpack hanging from the closet door hook, she paused, unable to stop herself from reaching out to touch the tags.

Tris had collected them from the various Swiss cantons where he'd played hockey. She had perfect recall of everything they'd talked about on the ship. Even after all these years, she still reeled from the flood of intimate memories assailing her. For a moment her eyes closed tightly in reaction.

At first she confused the warmth invading her body with those associations. Then she heard Tris murmur something unintelligible and realized it was his hands she felt gently touching her shoulders. The lower portion of his face was buried in her hair. "Are you all right?"

"I was just surprised to see it," her voice trembled.

Though he didn't know it, they'd stood like this before with his chest against her back. Now, as then, she could feel her heart pounding furiously. Tris couldn't help but be aware of her heightened emotions.

"If you want to read the letter you wrote to me, it's in my room," he said in a gravelly tone. "After we find Alain, I'll show it to you."

"I-it's not important," she stammered incoherently, making a valiant attempt to come to her senses. Another second and she would turn around to cover his mouth with her own.

Last night when he'd unexpectedly kissed her, she'd almost given in to the pressure of his mouth urging her to respond with more passion. She'd wanted to. He would never know how much! But she hadn't dared because he'd only been testing her, seeing what it was like to kiss her.

She knew Tris. He'd wanted to try and recapture the memories because after all, they'd once been lovers even if it had been for a very short period of time.

But if she were to kiss him now, he would know the depth of her feelings. The boy she'd given her heart and soul to had become a man, one whom she adored in brand new ways. As terrifying as it was to admit to herself, her love for Tris was more profound and intense than before.

It took every ounce of control to hold back her desire. Feeling slightly feverish, she eased away from him.

"If we're going to spend time in the mountains looking for him, I'd better change shoes and grab a pullover. It's going to rain."

On her way out of the room he called to her. "We may have to camp out all night so plan accordingly."

All night?

A shiver raced up her spine before Rachel hurried to the bedroom to get ready. Tris came in a few minutes later with his backpack. He put her extra clothes in with his.

"I asked Simone to fix us some food. You can carry it in Alain's spare pack."

She bit her lip. "He might not like the fact that I'm using it."

"Let me worry about that." His brusque comment revealed the depth of his concern over his nephew's disappearance. "I called Natalie and told her we might not be back until tomorrow."

Their daughter had been on her mind, too. "Did she sound upset?"

"Only in the sense that Alain was still missing. She seems perfectly content to remain with my parents."

"She's always been prepared to love you and your family," Rachel said before realizing she'd touched on the one subject that would keep Tris from forgiving her.

To her shock he didn't come back with some wounding retort. Thankful for his silence, she followed him down to the kitchen. He helped her on with the small pack.

"Thank you," she said, steeling herself not to react to the contact.

His fingers still tested the weight of the straps on her shoulders. "Is that comfortable?" He was standing so close, she could feel his warm breath on the back of her neck.

She weaved in place. "I-it's fine."

"Then let's go."

They descended to the storeroom where he expertly tied the tent bag and bedroll to his pack. Once that was accomplished they left the chalet and headed for the forest.

In a matter of minutes the tiny mountain village of Caux lay behind them. Though it was only midafternoon, the darkening clouds made it seem more like evening.

With each step Rachel marveled over the scenery. Every so often they came to a clearing in the pines where she could feast her eyes on snow capped peaks towering over green meadows, grazing cows and chalets hugging the hillsides.

"It's so beautiful, Tris, but I'm beginning to think we're not going to find Alain out here."

She heard him take a deep breath. "Why do you say that?"

"I've been trying to put myself in his shoes. I'm afraid the memories of being in this paradise with my family would be too painful for me to want to relive."

"You may be right," came the bleak reply, "but I won't stop looking until I've exhausted every possibility."

"I didn't mean—"

"I know what you meant, Rachel."

He kept going on those long powerful legs. She struggled to keep up, sensing how desperately he hoped this search wouldn't be in vain. More than anything Rachel wanted to believe they'd find Alain before the night was out.

But the deeper they penetrated the forest, the lower her spirits plunged. Regrets about the way she'd handled the past started to creep in worse than before.

If she'd contacted Tris years ago, none of this would be happening now. Alain and Natalie would have grown up together as cousins. There would have been acceptance.

Instead the news that Tris had a daughter had been thrust upon Alain without warning. The shock of learning she would be living with him and his uncle was asking too much of a boy still grief stricken over the loss of his parents.

"What's wrong, Rachel?" She lifted her head to discover Tris had stopped to drink from his water bottle. He stared at her through dark lashes, scrutinizing her features with disturbing intensity. "Am I hiking too fast for you?"

"No."

"Liar," he whispered, then handed her the bottle so she could quench her thirst. "Stop blaming yourself for a situation that's no one's fault."

There was little point in pretending she didn't know what he was talking about. She gave the bottle back, meeting his gaze head on. "Does this mean you've forgiven me a little?"

"How could I not?" his voice grated. "After the gift your mother gave me, many things have become clear."

She blinked. "My mother—what are you talking about?"

He put the bottle back in his pack, then flicked her a glance. "The pictures of us on the ship. The ones you took, I took, and someone else took of us. Your mother kept them after you threw them out."

Rachel gasped in shock.

"She asked Natalie to give them to me. What I saw helped me see what I couldn't have understood otherwise. We *were* very young and reckless, Rachel.

"When you didn't hear from me again, you had every right to think I was a guy who'd happened on to a good thing, and made the most of it for the time we were given.

"It's no wonder that having ended up an unwed mother, you felt you'd been abandoned by some arrogant hockey jock who'd found an appreciative audience aboard ship."

That was exactly how she'd felt.

"If I'm upset now, it's because I wasn't there to help you through your pregnancy. What you experienced without a husband couldn't have been easy no matter how wonderful your parents were. If anyone's to blame for this situation, I am."

"That's absurd," she blurted. "You had a near fatal accident."

He shook his head. "When I returned from New Hampshire, I had a long talk with my parents. Once their initial shock subsided, my father chastised me for my anger. He reminded me that if anyone was to blame, I was for sleeping with you before we were married. He was right. But I'm not sorry Natalie was the result."

Tris studied her features. "It's time to put the blame and anger behind us. Life's too short. I realized that when I discovered Alain missing this morning."

Rachel never expected to hear those words from him. Relief swept over her in waves. "We'll find him. How much farther is it to the camping spot you told me about?"

"Ten minutes. If we hurry, we'll beat the rain."

CHAPTER EIGHT

TRIS could have made it to the stream in five minutes, but because Rachel was along, it took more like fifteen. She felt raindrops and could hear thunder in the distance.

By the time they reached the camping spot, she was totally disheartened because there was no sign of Alain. They hadn't even seen another hiker to ask about him.

"I was hoping he'd be here."

"He might be camped further upstream. After the storm passes over, we'll go look for him." Tris sounded more in control than she felt.

In an economy of movement he set up the two man tent. It wasn't any too soon. As he was driving in the last peg, the deluge began in earnest.

He relieved her of her pack. "You first." With Tris's help lifting the flap, she crawled inside. He followed carrying both packs and a flashlight which he'd turned on. She took the food pack from him while he untied the sleeping bag and rolled it out. There was little room to maneuver.

Once they could sit on top of it, she pulled out sandwiches and fruit. Simone had provided a thermos of coffee which was still hot. Rachel poured some into the cup and handed it to him.

His food disappeared fast. So did hers. Not having eaten breakfast, she was starving.

The coffee tasted good. For dessert she bit into a ripe plum. It was sweet and juicy. Tris put out a finger to catch the juice dripping off her chin. As he raised it to his lips, their eyes met.

"What is it?" he asked in his low, vibrant voice.

"Nothing." She looked away quickly.

"I don't buy that. Something's going on."

He wouldn't rest until he had an answer.

"When you did that just now, it reminded me of the first night we had to stay in the cabin because of the hurricane. While the wind was howling outside our porthole, we sat safe inside on top of the bunk."

"Did we face each other like we're doing now?"

"Yes. Of course the ship was moving up and down and sideways. We had a struggle not to fall on the floor."

"So we held on to each other?" Suddenly he smiled. When Tris did that, she could hardly breathe.

"Yes. You'd brought us all kinds of goodies to snack on. I remember eating a peach. It was so juicy, you reached out so it wouldn't drip all over me."

"What else did I do?" he asked in a teasing voice before biting into an apple.

Heat filled her cheeks. "I'm sure your imagination can figure it out. We had about as much room in my cabin as we have in this tent."

A crack of thunder resounded unexpectedly. She flinched in surprise. Tris laughed. The sound brought back more memories that made her pulse race.

"I swear the elements are every bit as fierce as they were then."

"Don't be nervous," he murmured. "It's a summer storm and will blow itself out soon."

"That's what you told me on the ship!"

He cleared up their mess and put the little pack next to the big one against the wall of the tent. "Obviously we survived."

Now they were getting on dangerous ground. It was time to change the subject.

"I don't like to think of Alain out in this alone."

"Relax, Rachel. His father taught him how to take care of himself in the outdoors. He has a pup tent and sleeping bag. I'm convinced he's around here somewhere."

"You honestly believe that?"

"Yes. He loves these mountains. Thanks to your suggestions, we've covered all the other areas where he might have gone."

"What if he's hungry?"

"He probably took along a stash of protein bars. With those and a stream of water nearby, he can survive for a long time."

She shot him a covert glance. "I know you're trying to make me feel better, but I can't help worrying. He's only twelve."

"It's hard to believe only seven years separates him from the age I was when I first met you."

They were back to that again.

"I bet every guy at our table hated my guts."

"If they did, I was only aware of the English girl sitting next to you. When no amount of flirting on her part could persuade you to spend time with her, I was afraid she was going to come up behind me and push me overboard."

"It's evident I didn't give her a chance."

Rachel was starting to feel warm all over. "No. I'm afraid we pretty well ignored everyone."

A chuckle escaped his throat. "I believe in concentrating on one woman at a time."

"Have there been many since your recovery?" she asked, not wanting to know, but unable to stand it any longer not knowing. Being with him like this again had made her curiosity insatiable.

His eyes narrowed on her mouth. "A few."

"I have to admit I'm surprised you're not married."

"So's my mother." He expelled a breath.

"I have one of those, too."

"Our daughter appears to adore her. I must admit I'm looking forward to meeting her."

"For Natalie's sake mom always wanted you to know the truth. I did, too. But the thought of you being married with children and having to tell them…" Her voice trailed.

"I came close to marriage twice in my late twenties," he volunteered. "Before that the doctors warned me that if I were to play hockey again and receive another blow to my head, I probably wouldn't wake up. Deprived of enjoying my favorite sport, I'm afraid I spent my college years a very angry man. I dated some, but marriage was the last thing on my mind."

"I can understand that. You had such a passion for it, Tris. It doesn't surprise me it took you time to figure out where to channel all that competitive energy."

He nodded. "Papa liked my ideas for expansion and gave me free rein with that side of the business. I found the work challenging. Over time I had relationships with several women.

"In the one case, the attraction started out strong. But when I was away from her, I didn't miss her to the degree that she was my whole life. I eventually ended it.

"Later on I met another woman who appealed to me initially. But as time unfolded, I discovered she had a hard edge. When I thought of us having children, I couldn't see her being the best mother, so I broke it off."

"I can relate," Rachel murmured. "It's one thing to meet someone you're drawn to, but quite another to watch them interact with your child. Or not... Because of Natalie, I'm afraid I've been very critical of the men I've dated."

"Except for Steve."

She swallowed hard. "Yes. He's—"

"A wonderful man," Tris finished the thought. "So you've told me. Natalie seems to like him, too."

"She does." Rachel started to squirm. "What about your receptionist?"

"Suzanne?"

"If that's her name, then yes." The words came out jerkily. "When do you intend for Natalie to meet her?"

Tris changed positions so he could stretch out with his head propped. His rock-hard legs brushed the side of her hip and remained there. The rain continued to pour down, enclosing them in an intimacy that made her tremble.

"One of these days I'll take her to the office and introduce her to everyone."

Rachel tried to move to the side so she couldn't feel any physical contact with him. But she only made more room for him to sprawl against her.

"Does Suzanne know you have a daughter?"

"*Bien sur.* After I told my parents, I called my office staff together and explained the situation."

"What a shock that must have been to everyone."

"Let's put it this way. The revelation caused a minor earthquake at the Monbrisson Corporation."

"I knew it!" Rachel whispered.

"What do you think you know?" he demanded quietly.

"When Natalie's team won their championship, I almost called your office to tell you about her. The other fathers were there to congratulate their girls. But at the last second I lost my nerve because I didn't know what your reaction would be. The last thing I wanted to do was embarrass you."

He jackknifed into a sitting position, bringing him too close to her. "Embarrass me? *Mon Dieu,* don't you realize that knowing I have a daughter has brought me unspeakable joy?" His voice throbbed with emotion. "Guy still hasn't gotten over the fact that he played a part in getting us together."

"What about Suzanne?"

"What about her? My news put an end to any fantasies she might have entertained about us being a couple."

"I don't understand." By this time Rachel got to her knees to break the contact. "I thought— I mean you said something about Alain being threatened by her. I took it to assume you'd been dating her."

She couldn't read the expression in his dark eyes. "Suzanne has been my employee for four years. I'm afraid it's my mother who has nursed the hope I might see her in a more personal light. Unfortunately *Maman* made it known to Alain. When he questioned me about it, I put him straight."

The news that he wasn't involved with anyone shouldn't have excited Rachel so much.

"Did you notice the rain has stopped?" She jumped to her feet in order to get away from him. "Now we can look for him."

Crouching a little, she stepped past Tris's well honed male physique and emerged from the tent, gulping in the cool moist air.

"Wear this," Tris said a minute later. He was wearing a sweater, and handed her one of his hooded pullovers from the backpack.

"Thank you." Rachel put it on, aware of his eyes watching her. Though it drowned her, the dry warmth felt good.

She looked up at the sky. The rain might have let up, but there was no break in the clouds.

"It'll probably rain again before long." Tris read her mind. "Before that happens and it gets too dark, let's see if we can find him."

They worked their way through the wet ground cover bordering the stream. Rachel took turns with him calling out Alain's name. About a half mile from camp they met a group of German hikers. Tris switched to *schweitzer-deutsche* to communicate, displaying the same fluency with which he spoke English.

The men shook their heads. They obviously hadn't come across Alain.

Tris thanked them. When he turned to her, she wasn't surprised to see his face had darkened with lines. "Those hikers have been following the stream for several hours without seeing anyone else. The only thing for us to do is search below our camp."

Rachel nodded.

They doubled back, calling out Alain's name. Rachel could have wept because there was no answering cry. A half mile below the place where they'd set up their tent, she could smell rain in the air again.

"We'll have to resume our search in the morning," Tris muttered. "Come on. I'll race you to the tent."

She did her best to keep up with him, realizing the concern over Alain's disappearance was making them both a little frantic.

Not two minutes after their return, rain pelted the tent. While she discarded the damp pullover, Tris flicked on the flashlight to check his cell phone messages.

"Anything?" she asked.

He grimaced before saying no. The news caused her spirits to plummet. She could only imagine his state of mind.

Wanting to comfort him, she reached for the thermos and poured him the last bit of coffee. "Here. You need it."

Their gazes collided. "What about you?"

"None for me. Not at this time of night."

He took her at her word before drinking thirstily.

"There's more food."

"Maybe later." After putting the lid back on the thermos, he picked up the sleeping bag and unzipped it. "You're cold. If you'll find the space blanket I packed, we'll lie on it and put the sleeping bag over us."

Rachel tried hard to act normal as she did his bidding. They were two adults who'd formed a search party for Alain, nothing more.

What an ironic twist. At eighteen she'd displayed none of the signs of an hysterical virgin. She and Tris had loved each other, wanted each other. It had been so easy then, so natural. So wrong.

It was wrong now because she wanted him more than ever. They still weren't married.

Nervously she removed her sneakers and put them away in the corner. Tris waited for her to lie down, then stretched out next to her and covered them with the bag. Out went the light. She was alarmed to realize the rain had turned into a steady drizzle. Now he would be able to hear her heart thudding. She turned on her side away from him. He lay on his back with his hands beneath his head.

By the quiet on his part, she knew he was in agony over Alain. In truth, so was she. They needed to talk about it or go crazy.

"Tris?"

"Yes?" His voice sounded like it had come from a dark cavern.

"How did you break the news you had a daughter to Alain?"

She felt him change positions. He must have turned on his side toward her because she could feel new warmth.

"As soon as I arrived back from Concord, we hiked up here and camped out for a few days. It was in this tent I reminded him of the conversation we'd had before I went on military maneuvers. You wouldn't know, but he almost fell apart when I had to do my army stint.

"Anyway, after finding your letter and reading it to me, he asked me about Suzanne. I realized he was worried about her importance in my life. To put his mind at rest I told him not give it another thought because the right woman hadn't come along yet.

"His answer to that was, 'Maybe this Rachel

was the right one, and that's why you've never been able to love anyone else, even though you don't remember her.'"

Rachel's eyes smarted. Darling Alain.

"After I turned off the flashlight and we'd settled down, I told him his theory had been right. It seemed I *had* fallen in love with you, and out of that love you gave birth to our baby daughter."

Hearing Tris tell it caused her to sob. She felt his hand slide up her arm and gently caress her shoulder. It was a gesture meant to comfort. When she could get hold of her emotions she said, "How did he take the news?"

"By reminding me of the lecture I'd given him."

"What lecture?"

Tris made a strange sound in his throat. "Something about hormones getting you into trouble and making you a father before you were ready."

"You're kidding—" She half laughed, half cried.

"I thought he handled the news extremely well. He asked dozens of questions about Natalie and seemed quite delighted to think he had a cousin."

"You mean as long as she remained in America," Rachel interjected.

His hand tightened on her upper arm. "The minute I told him you weren't married, and that I'd invited you and Natalie to live with us for a year, that's when things started to go wrong. He didn't want to camp anymore. After we got back to the house he announced he was going to go live with the grandparents."

Rachel moaned. "He was shattered."

"I'm afraid he wasn't the only one."

"Did he move out?"

"Yes. It took me a week to talk him into coming back home. The situation was so fragile, I sent the plane for you and Natalie. Much as I wanted to come for you myself, I didn't dare. He refused to drive to the airport with me to pick you up."

Forgetting their proximity, she sat up to face him. "He's in crisis, Tris. I'm really frightened for him."

He turned onto his back once more. "As soon as we find him, I'm taking him for professional counseling. He's been through so much, I thought I could help him alone."

"While you get him the help he needs, Natalie and I are going back to Concord. Please listen—" she cried when he started to protest. "I don't mean permanently. Just until you achieve some kind of breakthrough with him."

"There's no telling how long that will take."

"True, but Natalie's totally secure in your love. Though she's young, she understands Alain is having such a hard time, he ran away. She'll be able to handle the separation from you because she'll know it's only temporary.

"Why don't we set up some plan of visitation that isn't so intrusive? It will give Alain time to accept Natalie as an integral part of your life. I'm aware you want to make up for lost time with her, but Alain can't handle it yet."

An emotion-filled silence followed.

"Where in the hell could he be?" Tris finally asked in a tortured voice. It didn't sound like he'd even listened to her suggestion.

She bowed her head. "He loves you so much, he won't stay away long wherever he is."

"If I don't hear something by morning, I'll call the police to help in the search."

A strange nuance in his voice caused Rachel to look down at him. It was too dark to see him, but she sensed something was wrong. Maybe it was the way he held his arm across his forehead. Like he was in physical pain.

Oh, no.

"You're having one of those headaches aren't you."

"I'll be fine."

"We don't have any ice, but I know something that might help to get you to sleep. Turn on your side away from me."

The fact that he obeyed meant he was in too much distress to argue with her.

"Just relax and let me do the work."

She cupped his neck, then started rotating her thumbs against the base of his skull. It was a trick her father had taught her. It sometimes worked with his patients who suffered from migraines. You had to know the exact spots to press. If done right, it opened up the constricted blood vessels in the head.

Since Tris had come back into her life, she finally had a legitimate reason to be touching him. It was a thrill to do anything for him. She lost track of the time. When she finally removed her hands, she could tell he'd fallen into a deep sleep.

Rachel silently thanked her father, then kissed the back of Tris's neck before lying down.

Her mind kept replaying that moment at the table when Alain ran out of the kitchen. His sudden departure from the table hadn't happened until hockey was mentioned.

There'd been another defining moment earlier in the day when Tris had praised Natalie for catching the only fish. The crushed look on

Alain's face still hurt Rachel when she thought about it.

In both cases the focus had been on Natalie's accomplishments. Clearly Alain hero worshipped Tris and wanted to shine in his uncle's eyes. But since he wasn't allowed to play hockey, and had no success fishing, he felt Natalie had usurped his place in his uncle's affection. No wonder he'd thought his world had come to an end.

She eventually fell into a troubled sleep. The next thing she knew, Tris was nudging her awake.

"Rachel? We have to get going."

Her eyelids fluttered open to discover him standing over her. He'd opened the tent flap to let in the morning air. She smoothed the hair away from her temples and got to her feet.

"I take it there's been no word of Alain," she said, putting on her shoes.

Tris shook his head. "I spoke to my father. He's already alerted the police." He tied up the sleeping bag and set it on top of his pack. "One of the officers is going to meet us at the chalet."

After putting on her pullover, she reached for the small backpack. "I'm ready." As she turned to leave, Tris unexpectedly caught her to him.

"You had angel fingers last night. It's the first

time since the accident I was out of pain within minutes," came his husky whisper. His eyes wandered over each feature. "*Merci,* Rachel." He kissed her thoroughly on the mouth before exiting the tent.

She touched fingers to her lips. Dazed by the experience, she stepped outside on wobbly legs. Tris was already removing the tent pegs, acting as if nothing important had happened. He could have no idea what his kiss had done to her. She loved him with an ache that would never, ever go away.

Attempting to act nonchalant, she helped him fold the tent. Once he'd attached it to his pack frame, he handed her their water bottle.

"Take a good long swallow."

She drank her fill, then gave it back. He packed it in one of the pockets. "Let's get going. It's all downhill."

The day was already a beautiful one. Only a few clouds dotted the sky. But without any word of Alain, it was a living nightmare. Tris paced his stride so she could keep up, but he was in no mood for talk. He couldn't. His pain was too debilitating.

Ten minutes later they came to the first clearing which gave out on a fabulous view. Tris stopped so they could drink. It gave her a minute to look around. In the distance she could see a little village to the right that hadn't been visible yesterday because of the clouds.

"What town is that?"

He looked in the direction she was pointing. "Les Avants."

"I didn't realize. The perspective's so different from here." That meant the Gorge Du Chauderon was nearby.

Was is at all possible Alain had camped there in order to catch fish? He'd been so determined the other day, and so disappointed when he'd had no bites.

"Tris, let's go back through the Gorge!"

His dark head swerved toward hers. "After what happened, why would he go there again?"

"It's just a guess, but he wanted to be the one who caught fish in front of you. He's in competition with Natalie. If he could bring home a catch of trout, then he'd get your praise. Don't you see?"

A light flickered in his gorgeous brown eyes, then went out. "I wish it were that simple."

"Maybe it is."

He rubbed the back of his neck anxiously. "If I thought he'd camped there…"

"Let's find out. Come on."

One small modicum of hope made a huge difference. They practically raced across the mountain toward the gorge. If Alain could see the look on his uncle's face right now, he would know how well loved and wanted he was.

Please be there, Alain.

They entered the top of the ravine and worked their way down through the heavy foliage. Rachel held her breath as they neared the area where they'd fished the other day.

When they reached the exact spot, she was devastated to discover no one was about. In agony she called out his name. No response.

Tears filled her eyes. She called to him again, but she was so choked up, very little sound came out.

"Alain! Mon fils! Ou es tu?" Tris's deep male voice ricocheted off the sides of the gorge. If Alain was in the vicinity, he would have heard it. *"Alain!"*

The white ring outlining Tris's taut mouth frightened her.

"Maybe he's camped further downstream."

Tris squeezed her shoulder before they forged ahead, following the same route they'd taken before. In this section of the ravine the stream wound serpentine style through the large outcroppings of rocks where small pools were created.

"Alain!" Tris shouted one more time.

"Par ici, mon oncle!"

The young voice they heard sounded heart-rendingly familiar. Then Alain appeared around a rock carrying eight good-size trout on a stick in one hand, his fishing gear in the other. He was dirty and tired, but there was the unmistakable glow of pride on his face as he walked toward his uncle.

Tris flashed her a look of joy mixed with some other emotions harder to decipher. She would think about that later. Right now all that mattered was Alain. He'd been found safe and well.

Rachel hung back to watch their reunion. She knew Tris was bursting to hug his nephew. But the first thing he did was stop in front of the trophies and make a gesture of surprise, spreading his arms.

"Oh la la, mon fils. C'est fantastique!" He took the stick from him and lifted it in the air. *"Bravo! Merveilleux!"* With one strong arm free, he gave his nephew a huge bear hug.

A joyous laugh came out of Alain.

She let them talk for a few minutes, then made an appearance, prepared to see Alain go back in his shell.

"I never saw anyone catch that many fish before. If your uncle has a camera back at the chalet, we'll get a picture to show your friends and grandparents."

His brows lifted. "Papa could catch this many."

"Well it's obvious you've inherited his skill. If you keep this up, I wouldn't be surprised if one day you're such a famous fly fisherman, people from all over will come to you for advice. You can call it the Alain Monbrisson Method."

That brought a smile to his lips.

Another smile lit Tris's eyes. "I think we'll have to stop by the office and show everyone. Guy *thinks* he's a good fisherman."

"Maybe after that we could all go out to celebrate. What's your favorite place in the world to eat, Alain?"

He looked from her to Tris. "Could we go to McDonald's?"

Of course. How was it she hadn't seen that coming?

"McDonald's it is," Tris said with a straight face. "First however, let's get these fish on ice. Where's your camp?"

"Near the bottom of the gorge."

"Then let's go."

Tris flashed her a silent message of gratitude before starting down the path with his hand on

Alain's shoulder. She stayed far enough behind that they could have a private conversation. At some point Tris would ask his nephew to leave a note the next time he decided to go camping on his own.

Before long they reached the chalet.

When Simone saw them coming, she raced down the steps to hug Alain like she would a favorite grandson. She made such a fuss of him and his spectacular catch, he was beaming.

Tris disappeared for a moment, then came back with a camera. He took enough pictures to fill half a scrapbook.

With a promise to be extra careful, Simone carried the fish inside to put them on ice. Rachel followed her up the stairs to the kitchen, After she emptied the small backpack and thanked the housekeeper for the food, she hurried to the bedroom for a shower.

"Rachel?" Alain whispered.

She spun around in surprise. "What is it, honey?" The endearment came out naturally.

"Did you tell Uncle Tris about the flies?"

The flies?

Oh. The *flies*.

"*What* flies?"

He stared at her for at least ten seconds. Then he darted her a little smile and left the room.

Maybe it was too soon, but in her heart she believed Alain and Tris's relationship had turned a corner for the better. That meant she and Natalie could go home to Concord today.

Once she told Natalie everything, her daughter would understand. With the cooperation of Tris's parents, they would head for Geneva while Tris took Alain to his office to show him off.

CHAPTER NINE

TRIS pulled the car to a stop at the side entrance of his parents' house. He could see his mother pulling weeds in the garden. Alain climbed out first and ran over to her. Tris followed.

How odd that his father's car was gone. It surprised him. The plan had been that the whole family would go out to eat as soon as he and Alain got back from the office.

He presumed Rachel was inside with Natalie, telling her about their harrowing experience, one that magically turned out to have a happy ending thanks to Rachel.

"Grand-mere? We're back!"

She glanced around at Alain and got to her feet. Still wearing her gardening gloves, she hugged him. "What did Guy say when he saw all those fish?"

"He couldn't believe it. He thought I'd bought them at the *poissonnerie*."

She patted her hands against her legs and laughed.

"I told him to come fishing with me next time and I'd prove that I caught them myself."

"Where's everyone?" Tris asked quietly.

"Your father took Natalie and her mother to Geneva. They wanted to see the school she attended. I don't think they expected you back quite this soon. You know—once you're there you're inclined to talk business."

Everything his mother said made sense, yet he had the gut feeling something was wrong.

"Can we go to McDonald's now?"

"Absolutely." She hugged Alain again. "I'm hungry."

"Me, too," he declared emphatically. "Aren't you, Uncle Tris?"

Up until five seconds ago Tris had been looking forward to everything he'd planned out for the rest of the day.

"Since we don't know how soon they'll return, it makes no sense to put off lunch." He and Alain had only been gone an hour.

It was an hour's drive to Geneva. According to his calculations, they couldn't possibly be back for another hour and a half, not if they intended to visit the school.

"Give me a minute to go inside and get my purse," his mother said. "Then we'll leave." She hurried off.

Again he got to the distinct impression she'd avoided looking at him. Alain walked to the car and got in the back seat to wait.

Obeying blind instinct, Tris pulled out his cell phone to call his father. He cursed when all he got was his voice mail. In the next instant he saw his mother and intercepted her on the porch steps.

"What's going on, Maman?"

She looked up at him with loving eyes. "I think you already know." Her hands curled around his arm to prevent movement. "Before you react, I have to tell you we all had a long talk. I think Rachel did the right thing to take Natalie back to Concord."

"How could it be right?" he snarled, removing his arm from her grasp.

"Rachel said she discussed setting up reasonable visitation with you last night."

"It wasn't a discussion," he said through tight lips.

"Are you telling me she lied?"

He bowed his head, attempting to tamp down

his anger. "She mentioned it, but there was no agreement."

"She's right, Tris. Alain is threatened by Natalie. I know you want everything to fit together perfectly all at once. It's your nature, and it has worked for you in business.

"But this situation is entirely different. Rachel has a very level head on her shoulders. She's trying to do the best thing by you, Alain—and your daughter. If it helps, your daughter was amazingly mature about the decision to leave, and that's all due to her remarkable mother."

To hear his mother *say* it, was remarkable.

His eyes closed tightly. Rachel was so much more than he could explain in words. Since her arrival in Switzerland, he'd become a different man.

"Uncle Tris? How come you're taking so long?"

"You see how he needs you?" his mother implored him.

Yes he saw. But Tris had needs, too.

Needs that had been buried when an accident wiped out his memory. Though those precious cells were gone forever, other brain cells had been busy storing new memories teeming with possibilities that sent his blood racing.

"We're coming." He grasped his mother's arm and helped her down the steps to the car.

Forty-five minutes later they returned to the house. Alain had satisfied his appetite with fast food his grandparents normally disdained.

No sooner did Tris shut off the motor and get out than he saw his father's car coming in the driveway. He pulled up next to Tris and opened the car door.

Their eyes met in silent acknowledgment that Rachel's mission had been accomplished. By now the jet would have attained cruising speed. An emptiness stole through him so gut wrenching, he groaned.

"Hey, where's everybody?" Alain asked his grand-pere.

Tris hadn't thought his nephew would even notice.

"Well—" His father got all the way out of the car and shut the door. "After we drove by Rachel's old school, I took them to the plane."

"Plane—where did they go?"

"Back to New Hampshire," Tris answered for his parents.

"Huh?" Alain spun around. He looked up at Tris in bewilderment.

The last thing his nephew needed was to think he was responsible for this latest change in plans. As far as Tris was concerned, their leaving was Tris's own personal crisis. One he needed to work through without alarming Alain.

"Last night Rachel found out something important had happened at her work. She needed to get back to her job and her boyfriend. Natalie decided to go with her so she wouldn't be alone. They'll come again. Probably during their Thanksgiving Holiday in November."

Alain looked shocked. "But I thought they were going to stay a whole year."

"At the time it sounded like it might work, but things have a way of changing. Since they're gone and I have the time off, why don't you and I plan a little trip somewhere fun. We'll talk about it on the way back to the house."

"Okay."

Tris eyed his parents one more time before getting in the car. Alain hugged them, then joined him. His nephew was unusually silent en route to Caux.

"You must be thinking hard, *mon gars*. Have you come up with any ideas yet?"

"No."

"What about London?"

"I went there with Maman and Papa."

"How about Greece? We could go to one of the islands for a beach vacation."

Alain turned his head to look at him. "Is that what you want to do?"

"Who doesn't love the beach?" Tris came back.

"But you don't really want to go there."

"What makes you say that, Alain? As long as we're together, I don't care where we are."

By the time they'd arrived at the chalet, Tris had reached such a low point, he didn't know where to turn.

His nephew studied him intently. "Are you crying over me?"

He blinked back the tears without giving Alain a verbal answer. Too many gut wrenching emotions were surfacing right and left.

"Of course over you," Tris answered finally in a gruff tone. "I don't believe you have any idea of how much I love you. I got sick to my stomach when I couldn't find you. How would you feel if I just disappeared and wasn't in any of the places you searched?"

"Awful," Alain admitted. "I love you, too, Uncle Tris." He reached over and hugged him so hard, he almost cut off his breathing. "I'm sorry I didn't tell you I went fishing. I won't ever do that again. I promise."

"I believe you. Now let's forget it and just enjoy ourselves from now on. Do you want to play video games this afternoon? Maybe I can beat you this time."

With his head still resting against Tris's arm he said, "Could I ask you another question?"

"Anything."

"Do you think we could go to Concord for a vacation?"

Tris's thoughts reeled. Where had *that* come from? "You *want* to?"

"I wish you'd taken me with you the first time, but you said you had to go alone."

Incroyable.

If he was reading his nephew correctly, the greatest damage in this whole nightmare had been done by leaving his nephew behind.

Of course! *Alain* had been the one to find the letter. He'd cracked the mystery. *He'd* been the person to suggest Tris could never love anyone else but Rachel. He'd assumed that he and Tris were a team, then Tris had done the unthinkable and had left Alain behind.

"I should have taken you with me," he confessed emotionally. "I'll never leave you again."

"You love her, huh."

"Natalie's my daughter. You're my son now. I love both of you."

"I know that," Alain exclaimed as if he'd always known it and couldn't understand why Tris didn't. "I'm talking about Rachel."

His nephew continually astounded him. "How do you know that?"

"Because you look at her the way Papa used to look at Maman."

Was that right—

Tris's elation was off the charts. "Since you're so observant, young man, then you've also noticed she has a boyfriend she couldn't wait to get home to."

"You don't have to worry about Steve."

He blinked. "How come?"

"Natalie told me a secret."

When had *that* happened? What else didn't he know that had gone on under his own roof?

"If it's a secret, then I'm not supposed to hear it."

"You'll want to hear this. Her mom told her she could never love anyone the way she loved you."

Tris shook his head. "That was a long time ago. She said it in the heat of the moment."

"Why don't you ask Rachel to marry you and find out?"

His heart kicked so hard, the impact almost knocked him over. He stared incredulously at his nephew. "How would you feel about that?"

"Fine."

Fine?

"Do you want to know another secret?"

"Forget what I said about secrets. I'm all ears."

"When you were in the chocolate factory, Rachel took me to the village to buy some hand-tied flies from an expert. I wouldn't have been able to catch all those fish if she hadn't thought of it. She bought me pizza and paid for everything, too.

"She's nice, Uncle Tris. And beautiful, too," he added. "I can see why you loved her when you were on the ship."

After trying to catch his breath for the second time Tris said, "I've got an idea. Let's go in the house and plan our strategy."

"Natalie? Are you and Kendra ready to go to Nana's, honey? Steve will be here in a few minutes."

"Yup."

Yup. When Natalie started to talk in one word sentences, Rachel knew she was hurting.

During the drive to Geneva yesterday, she'd put on a brave face in front of her grandfather. But once they'd boarded the private jet, she'd broken down sobbing.

Rachel had stayed home with her today. They'd done the wash and a little cleaning. Before Kendra came over, they'd done a lot of talking.

Natalie's mind understood Alain's fear of losing Tris. It was her heart that suffered over the separation from her father. He hadn't phoned her yet, but it was only six-thirty in the evening.

Since finding out they'd left the country, he'd probably spent every minute with Alain trying to make him feel more secure. Still, Rachel had no doubt he'd find time to touch base with Natalie before she went to bed. If he didn't, Alain wasn't going to be the only child in the Monbrisson household who was in unbearable pain.

As for Rachel, she had her own private agony to sort out. If being with Steve tonight didn't do anything to assuage it, then she would have to break it off with him. He'd sounded too happy when she'd called him at work this morning and told him they'd come back earlier than planned.

Feeling the way she did about Tris, she couldn't imagine being able to love another man. Who would ever compare?

But as her mother had told her on the phone earlier today, the years had a way of flying by. Before she knew it, Natalie would be grown up and married. If Rachel didn't want to end up going through life alone, she owed it to her own happiness to try to make it work with Steve. In the event that didn't pan out, then she needed to try again with someone else.

Her mother was right.

Rachel looked in the mirror one more time to apply lipstick and a touch of green eye shadow to highlight her eyes. After blow-drying her hair, she left it loose and falling from a side part.

Steve had said to wear something dressy. In honor of tonight she'd chosen to wear her black dress with the square cut neck, simple yet chic. In taking extra care with her appearance, maybe it would infect her with a little excitement for an evening out with him. She hadn't seen him in a week.

When the doorbell rang, she found herself hoping the sight of him would stir her senses, or make her breath catch. Something—anything to prove she wasn't indifferent to him.

"I'll get it, Mom!"

"Thank you!"

She slipped on her strappy black heels and reached for the matching evening bag.

Halfway down the stairs she heard Natalie cry out, *"Dad!"*

Rachel's legs almost buckled. She clung to the banister. *Tris was here?*

Voices drifted up the staircase. Natalie was making introductions. Unless Rachel's hearing was faulty, she thought she heard Alain say hello to Kendra.

The buzzer rang again.

A second later, "Mom? It's Steve!"

No… This couldn't be happening.

"I—I'm coming, honey."

With a knot in her stomach, Rachel somehow managed to join the group congregated in her living room. She arrived in time to see the men shaking hands.

Rachel had known this day was coming. But not this soon.

Her gaze flew to Tris whose potent male physique looked impossibly elegant in a polo shirt and jeans. He flashed her an all encompassing glance, causing Steve to look around.

A silent cry rose in her throat because Tris's presence had blinded her to anyone else in the room.

"Steve—" She tried to act excited he'd come. "I—I see you and Natalie's father have met."

"That's right." He walked toward her with a smile, but it didn't reach his eyes. "You look beautiful," he whispered, giving her a kiss on the cheek. He'd worn a tan suit. With his dark blond hair, he'd never looked better himself.

"Thank you," she whispered back in an unsteady voice.

"I didn't realize he was in town."

Everyone was watching the two of them. "N-neither did I. Have you met Alain?"

"Not yet."

"Steve Clarkson? This is Alain Monbrisson, Natalie's cousin." She took the needed steps to reach him. Whether Alain liked it or not, she put an arm around his shoulders. She couldn't help it. She loved Tris's nephew.

"How do you do," Alain said politely and shook Steve's hand.

"Are you the one who caught all those fish?"

Bless you, Steve.

"Yes."

"I don't know how you do it. I'm impressed."

"You have to have the right flies." His blue eyes swerved to Rachel as if to ask if it was still their secret. She simply smiled back.

Steve chuckled. "I'll remember that when I take Rachel fishing."

"Mom?"

Trembling under Tris's unrelenting scrutiny, Rachel turned to her daughter. "Yes, honey?"

"Dad decided to spend the rest of his vacation here in Concord. He's rented the town-house two doors down."

What?

"Can Kendra and I go over there instead of Nana's? They're going to order pizza. Alain's never had American pizza before."

Tris put his hands on Natalie's shoulders. "If you two are going to be out late, why not let the girls stay over with us. I had the place furnished so there are plenty of beds."

How could he have accomplished everything so fast?

But Rachel already knew the answer to that question before she'd asked it. He was the head of the Monbrisson empire, a man able to move mountains without even thinking about it.

"Could we, Mom?"

"We'll probably go to a movie after we eat," Tris explained. "If Kendra's parents are in agreement, I'll run her home some time tomor-row."

"It'll be fine with them," Kendra assured him. She looked as mesmerized by Tris as Nat-alie.

The announcement that he'd actually carried through with his intention of renting the other townhouse had robbed Rachel of the ability to think coherently.

"Natalie? You'll have to call Nana and tell her you're not coming."

"I will."

"Y-you have a hockey game at ten."

"I know. We'll take our stuff to Dad's."

Steve reached out to tousle Natalie's hair. "I'm planning to be there, kiddo."

"That settles it," Tris spoke up in his deep voice. "We'll all go to support the Cavalry. Come on, everybody. I don't know about you, but I'm starving."

The kids were equally exuberant and hurried out the door ahead of Tris with their gear. He paused in the opening. "Have a good evening you two."

After flashing her a dark unreadable glance, he closed the door behind him, leaving a quivering Rachel to face Steve in the aftermath.

He stood there with his arms folded, staring at her through wounded eyes.

"I swear I didn't know he'd come to Concord, Steve."

"I believe you. Would you rather we called off dinner?"

"No. Of course not."

"I think it would be best."

"It's okay, really—"

He frowned. "When we started to date, I

knew I had a formidable opponent, otherwise you would have been married a long time ago. But I'd hoped that in time your memories of him would fade enough for you to let me in.

"Now that I've met Natalie's father and have felt the tension between you two, I can see that you'll never get over him."

Rachel turned to him, fighting tears. "I'm so sorry, Steve. I never meant to hurt you."

"I know that, but some things are beyond our control. He's one of them. It isn't as if he did something that turned off your love. The accident only put your relationship on hold. Now he's back in your life again. I can't fight that."

"You mean Natalie's life," she corrected him.

"You're an integral part of hers. Seeing all of you together has clarified things for me." She could hear it coming. "I'm going to bow out while I still can."

"Steve…"

"There's never been an end to your story. Until there is, no man has a chance with you. You're one terrific woman. I wish I'd met you first." After pressing a hard kiss to her cheek, he left the house.

She heard his car start up and drive away.

A hot tear trickled down her cheek. There was no finer man than Steve. But heaven help her, he wasn't Tris!

She dashed upstairs and collapsed on the bed, utterly convulsed. Her whole life seemed to play before her. She should never have gone to Europe the first time. Or if she had, not by water.

What forces had conspired to place her and Tris on the same ship, in the same class, at the same table?

As terrible as it was that Natalie hadn't known her father before now, it didn't compare to the tragedy that had befallen Alain. It wasn't fair he had to compete for Tris's love.

She could have told Steve that Tris wasn't in love with her. Right now Tris was trying desperately to keep his nephew from falling into a depression he might not be able to shake. Though Alain hadn't come off acting morose tonight, deep down he was suffering.

Tris made a big mistake in coming here for a vacation. Alain was so jealous of Natalie's place in his life, Rachel didn't want to think about the hockey game in the morning. Taking Alain to that match would be like pouring acid on an open wound.

She flung herself over on her back, staring up at the ceiling through blurry eyes. Where was it all going to end? She was dreading tomorrow.

* * *

Rachel had no idea which car in the skating rink parking lot was Tris's rental. After tossing and turning all night debating whether to come, it was her fault she had trouble finding an empty space. She glanced at her watch. Quarter after ten. The first period of the match would already have been played.

When she went inside, they were cleaning the ice before the next period started. The bleachers didn't hold very many people and there was only one set of them at the side of the rink. Parents and family members were packed together, yet she spotted Tris immediately.

Not because he sat front and center with Alain. Not because of his striking looks and stature. Not because he was wearing a black turtleneck that gave off a male sensuality to every woman in the crowd.

He had an intangible aura, a magnetic appeal. Call it whatever you wanted, Tris possessed it in abundance. She'd felt its pull on the ship years ago. And she still felt it now. Natalie and Alain worshipped at his feet.

That kind of response from male or female, young and old alike, proved he was an exceptional man.

Steve's words still haunted her. Until there was an end to the story, she was stuck in place, unable to progress. Speaking of place, one of the mothers she knew saw her and patted the spot next to her on the aisle. Rachel hurried up the steps to grab it before someone else did.

"Thanks, Judith."

"You're welcome. My husband had to leave."

"How are the girls doing?"

"No score for either side yet, but I think the Posse is playing more aggressively."

"Uh-oh. That's not g—"

"Rachel?"

Her heart jumped at the sound of Tris's voice. He must have seen her come in.

She turned her head. Their gazes collided. His dark eyes wandered from her hair which she'd tied back at the nape with another scarf, to the cream top and brushed denim jeans she'd chosen to wear.

"Where's Steve?"

"A problem came up at his work." It was a lie, but she wasn't about to tell him the truth in front of everyone.

"Then come and sit with me and Alain. We saved places for both of you."

So saying, he caught her around the hips and lifted her to the ground in a fluid motion only someone of his size and power could carry off.

Their bodies brushed against each other, sending an electric shock through her system.

"Judith?" Rachel's voice came out shakily. "I'll see you later."

Her astonished friend was staring so hard at Tris, she forgot to speak. He nodded to the other woman, then put his hand on the back of Rachel's waist to guide her to the front.

She recognized that possessive touch. If she closed her eyes, she could imagine herself back on the ship. He hadn't liked the attention the other guys paid her. She'd secretly loved his proprietorial behavior when he guided her out of the dining room to pursue more intimate pleasures.

To break the tension she said, "I hear Natalie's team isn't doing so well."

"Sometimes it takes until the final period to figure out your opponent."

"Tris? W-we have to talk."

"We already did the other night. You were right about not pushing everything all at once. Alain didn't mind the idea of coming here for a few days visit."

"Then why did you rent the townhouse? You could so easily have stayed at a hotel."

"I want him to get used to it in case you end up marrying Steve."

His comment wounded her in a whole new way. It appeared he'd already concluded her relationship with Steve would culminate in marriage. If ever she needed proof Tris had no romantic interest in her, he'd just given it to her.

"What does one thing have to do with the other?"

"Natalie told me Steve sells insurance. He can't very well leave all his clientele to move to Switzerland. I, on the other hand, can establish my headquarters anywhere I wish so I can be with our daughter. I'm simply planning ahead, covering every contingency."

That's what Tris did better than anyone else. He studied all the options before coming up with a solution no one could override. He'd meant what he'd said about moving here if there was no other way.

But the best solution for him was the worst for Rachel. To live two doors away from him until Natalie had grown up would mean she'd never get over him. The thought absolutely terrified her.

Alain saw them coming. "Hi, Rachel."

"Hi, yourself."

Tris pulled her down next to him with Alain on his other side. She leaned forward to look at him. "How was the pizza last night?"

"I think it's a lot better than the kind we have at home."

What an irony. Switzerland probably had some of the best food in the world. She was about to ask him how he liked the movie, but the teams had come back out on the ice.

Natalie waved to her. This had to be a special moment for their daughter. Both her parents sitting together to watch her play. Rachel waved back.

The second period got underway. The girls might only be Peewees, but they'd learned a lot since their first season and displayed real improvement.

"Natalie handles herself on the ice with amazing confidence," Tris murmured.

"I started her ice skating six years ago."

"It shows."

"So does her killer instinct. That comes from you."

She'd thought her comment would please him. Instead she felt a stillness steal over him as he watched Natalie tearing up and down the ice. Rachel couldn't begin to fathom what was going on in his mind.

At the end of the second period, Tris and Alain went to the concession stand to bring back drinks. She breathed a sigh of relief that

Alain appeared not to mind being a spectator. To Rachel's chagrin *she* was the one who was having problems. Her heightened awareness of Tris made it pure torture to sit by him and pretend she wasn't affected.

After a no scoring game so far, the third period started off with a vengeance. The competition had grown fierce.

Natalie showed the Monbrisson aggressiveness that had earned her one of the wing positions on the team. She was going all out for a win to show off for her father. Rachel feared she was taking too many risks.

Tris must have thought so, too. Several times she saw his hands form fists on his hard thighs.

By rights Natalie should have scored, but the opponents' goalie made some exceptional saves. While the Posse fans cheered, the fans for the Cavalry voiced their disappointment loudly.

When the opposition scored the only point in the last few seconds of the game, Rachel and Tris groaned at the same time. Not because the Cavalry had lost the game, but because their daughter had to face defeat in front of her brilliant father.

Some of the kids skated over to the sidelines. Among them she saw Kendra talking to her parents. Not Natalie. She skated off the ice without once looking in their direction. Rachel felt her dejection.

A concerned looking Tris got to his feet. "If you two don't mind, I'm going to find Natalie. We'll meet you at the car."

She turned to Alain, afraid his feelings would be hurt. "Would you like to ride home with me? That way Tris can bring Natalie when she's ready."

He nodded. "Okay."

His positive response surprised and relieved her.

"We'll see you in a few minutes, *mon gars.*" Tris gave his nephew's shoulder a squeeze. Flicking Rachel a worried father glance, he took off for the locker room.

"Let's go, shall we?"

On the way out of the rink they dropped their empty cups in the trash can near the entrance.

"How come Steve's not with you?" Alain asked after they started for home.

"At the last minute there was a problem at his work."

"Oh."

"Would you like to stop for ice cream?"

"Yes. Do they have strawberry?"

"They have fifty-one different flavors."

He cocked his head. "Fifty-one—"

"That's right. My favorite is chocolate chip cookie dough."

"What's that?"

She smiled. "You're about to find out."

A half hour later while they were enjoying ice cream back at the townhouse, Rachel heard the front door open.

"Mom?"

Alain glanced at Rachel.

"In the kitchen." She put her spoon down. Before she could reach the doorway, Natalie and Tris walked in. One look at her daughter's downcast face and she knew it wasn't good. She couldn't decipher Tris's expression.

"You played a wonderful game, honey."

"No, I didn't," Natalie said, avoiding a hug. "They shouldn't have been able to make that last shot."

"Your team's goalie should have stopped it," Alain piped up.

"Yeah, but it was my fault for not cutting her off before she could set up that shot."

"Next time go around her other side where she's not expecting you to be. Uncle Tris says that's the way to take them out."

Rachel watched in shock to see that Natalie was listening to Alain. Her daughter unconsciously helped herself to the ice cream from the fridge. In a minute they were having a big discussion about the game.

Tris unexpectedly put a hand beneath Rachel's hair. He whispered against her cheek, "Since the two of them seem to be sorting things out on their own, let's leave them to it."

She broke away from him and hurried into the living room. He was treating her like a wife. Rachel supposed it was because they were in the unique position of parenting their daughter together. But if he continued to touch her, he was going to get a wife's response. It would be distasteful to him and mortify her.

Feeling nervy and vulnerable, she sat down on the end of the couch, tucking her legs beneath her. He remained standing.

"Tris? How do you feel about Natalie playing hockey?"

He shot her a level gaze. "The truth?"

"Of course."

"It worries the hell out of me."

"I wondered if that's why you were quiet at the game. It's got me worried, too. Last year it seemed innocent enough, but she's matured a lot, grown stronger. So have the other girls.

"They play like guys! One of these days someone's going to get hurt. I can understand why

Bernard and Francoise didn't want Alain to have anything to do with it." Tears stung her eyes. "When I think of what happened to you—"

"*Rachel*—" his voice grated.

She buried her face in her hands. "I—I couldn't stand it if I lost her, too."

CHAPTER TEN

Too?

Tris's heart bounced against the walls of his chest.

Such a little word. But the reason Rachel had said it could mean the difference between heaven and hell for him.

She lifted her head, unaware of his excitement. "I wanted to help Natalie have an identity by telling her about your hockey career." Her words came out on a half-sob. "Instead I'm afraid I've set something in motion I already regret."

"Hey, Mom? Dad?" Natalie rushed in the living room, interrupting them. "Alain and I are going to go over to the other townhouse and watch the rest of the video we rented."

Rachel cleared her throat. "That's fine, honey."

Tris handed Alain the key. "See you guys later."

No sooner did Natalie open the door than Tris heard their daughter cry, "Nana!"

"Hello, darling. Who's this?"

Rachel's shocked gaze flew to Tris while they listened to the conversation on the porch.

"It's my cousin, Alain Monbrisson. This is my nana, Vivian Marsden."

"How do you do, Mrs. Marsden."

"I've been anxious to meet you, Alain. I'm tickled to death you two are related. When I was young, I just loved being with my cousins."

"It's fun." Alain said it like he meant it. Nothing could have pleased Tris more. His comment must have surprised Rachel. She jumped to her feet, brushing at the wetness glistening her cheeks.

"I'm sorry I had to miss your game, darling. Did you win?"

"No, but we will next time. See you later, Nana. We're going over to Dad's townhouse to watch a movie."

Tris stepped to the door. "At last we meet, Mrs. Marsden," he said as Rachel's mother came in the house. She was blond and hazel eyed. He studied her for a long moment. "Now I know where your daughter inherited her attractive looks."

She smiled. "Now I know where Natalie inherited *hers*. Thank you for the lovely flowering plant you sent me."

He took her hand in both of his. "It was the least I could do after the gift you gave me through Natalie. It has filled in the void left by my accident. I feel whole again, and totally indebted to you."

"You suffered. I'm sorry." Her compassion prompted him to lean down and kiss her on both cheeks. "My parents want to meet you. When Alain and I fly back in a few days, we'd like you to come with us."

Her eyes twinkled like his father's sometimes did. "I'll have to get a passport first. I think maybe I'll see about that this afternoon." She looked at her daughter. "I didn't realize Tris had flown in. Under the circumstances, I'm going to leave."

"Don't go, Mom!"

Tris heard panic in her voice. Rachel had been on edge since showing up at the rink. Before long he intended to know the reason why.

"We'll have plenty of time to talk later, darling."

"Then I'll walk you out."

Rachel swept past Tris without looking at him. He watched her accompany her mother to the car parked in front. If she was prevailing on her to stay, it didn't appear to be doing any good. Vivian got behind the wheel and drove off in short order.

Much as Tris would have liked to visit with Natalie's grandmother, he had to admit he was glad she left. He wanted certain answers from Rachel. Now that they were strictly alone, he would get them.

Once she came back inside, he said, "I get the feeling something else is wrong besides your concern that hockey's too dangerous for our daughter. Is it because Steve couldn't come with you?"

She folded her arms, a sure sign she didn't like his question.

"What are you afraid of, Rachel? You're behaving like you did on the phone when I first called you."

Her chin lifted mutinously. "I don't mean to be rude, but Steve isn't your business."

"He is if he's going to become Natalie's stepfather," Tris retorted. "Last night he couldn't wait to get you alone. It's obvious he's practically standing on his head to get close to Natalie. Which makes me even more curious why you came to the game alone. Tell me what's going on."

"It's not that simple, Tris. Steve and I haven't dated that long."

"It doesn't take long when it's the real thing," he challenged. "By the time you and I had eaten our first meal together, we knew there was something between us so strong and deep, nothing could have torn us apart except a catastrophe."

"That was different."

"You mean because we were young and reckless?" he baited her.

Between dark lashes her eyes flashed like green gemstones in sunlight. "Yes!"

"You've told me that before. I told Alain the same thing when he found your letter. Nevertheless we both know we fell madly in love and planned our wedding before we ever got off the ship.

"Now I need to know how close you are to making wedding plans with Steve. I came here with Alain to get things settled. He's doing much better, but the children don't need any more upheaval in their lives."

"You think I don't know that?" she cried.

"Judging by the pain in your voice, I take it you've already told Steve yes, and are worried about how this is all going to work out. So I'll try to make this easier for you.

"If you're going to move in with him, I'll buy the townhouse I've rented. But if Steve's moving in with you, then I'll purchase a home in Concord. One that's far enough away to put the children in different schools and give you and your husband privacy."

"No, Tris—"

She'd said no one too many times to him. "Sorry, Rachel, but you had it all your own way for twelve years. Now it's my turn."

"You don't understand." She shook her head. "You don't need to rent the townhouse or buy a house. None of that's necessary."

A tight band constricted his breathing. "Why not?"

"Because Steve doesn't want to marry me."

"Not according to Natalie!"

"Our daughter was with *you* last night. She doesn't know what happened after you all left."

"What did Steve do? Threaten to walk away if I tried to exercise my rights as Natalie's father? You want me to talk to him? Reassure him that I'll do everything possible to make this work?"

"No—" She spread her hands in silent entreaty. "It wasn't like that. He senses Natalie loves you too much to ever accept him."

Tris hadn't expected to hear that explanation. "She likes him well enough."

"Come on, Tris. We both know how she feels

about you. Our situation is so unique, no man's going to try to compete. It just wouldn't work."

Grace a dieu. "So what are saying?"

"If you want Natalie to live with you in Switzerland forever, then so be it. I happen to know it has always been her heart's desire. But as we both know, she'll never be happy without me. Therefore, I—I'm prepared to move there and find a job. Maybe I can talk my mother into moving there, too.

"I'll have to put the townhouse up for sale in order to buy something comparable in Montreux. That way we'll be able to share our daughter and you won't have to uproot Alain."

His adrenalin surged. "There's only one way to do this. That's for us to get married. We'll adopt Alain as our son so he feels as much a part of us as Natalie does."

Her face paled. "You're not serious—"

"Once upon a time we were lovers," he declared forcefully. "Natalie's our flesh and blood daughter. Alain needs a mother's influence. By rights you're his aunt and the perfect person to fill that role."

"Stop it, Tris. What you're suggesting is impossible."

"Why? Because you're still in love with Steve? I thought you were prepared to put Natalie's happiness above every other consideration."

Her body tautened. "I thought I just did. What we haven't talked about are *your* feelings."

"You already know what they are. The children are my first priority."

"I'm referring to your personal life. Some day the right woman will come along."

"I think Alain had it right the first time. The love I felt for you prevented me from falling for anyone else. When you think about it, who else but you already has a bond with Alain? He and Natalie share Monbrisson blood."

Hot color streamed into her cheeks. "But we're not the same people who fell in love on that ship."

"No we're not. We've both struggled a great deal since then. We've lost loved ones. Obviously we can't go back and change anything. But we could sure as hell try to make a wonderful life for the children. They're beginning to like each other."

"Alain would never accept me."

"You're wrong." Tris eyed her through shuttered lids. "That day in Broc, you did something for him that went soul deep. If he hadn't wanted to come on this trip, he would have stayed with the grandparents."

She didn't say anything.

As the silence grew, the smell of victory faded.

It was entirely possible that for once in his life, those gut instincts he'd always relied on were way off. Too late he realized his body had broken out in a familiar cold sweat.

"Think about it and let me know. I'm going to check on the kids."

After Tris walked out, Rachel stood there reeling over what he'd just said.

That day in Broc, you did something for him that went soul deep.

It meant Alain had told him about the flies. If that was true—and apparently it was since there would have been no other way for Tris to find out—then Alain did like her a little bit. Enough to come on this trip with Tris of his own accord.

So that left Tris… He still hadn't told her how he felt about her. How could she possibly give him a definitive answer until she knew the truth?

After vacillating for a little while, she couldn't stand it any longer and hurried over to the townhouse to have it out with him.

When she entered the living room, she found the kids sitting on the floor in front of the TV talking quietly. They'd turned off the video. Something was wrong.

She looked around. "Where's Tris?"

"He's upstairs lying down," Alain said.

"I made an ice pack for him with a wash-cloth," Natalie explained. "He told us to stay here until he'd slept it off."

"I'll look in on him to see if he's all right."

Rachel stole up the staircase. The townhouse was just like hers. She headed instinctively for the master bedroom.

A soft cry caught in her throat to see Tris stretched out on the bed. His handsome face looked drawn. There were smudge marks beneath his eyes. The dark lashes of his closed lids stood out against the pallor of his skin.

It was frightening to think a migraine could incapacitate a person so fast. Especially someone as mentally and physically strong as Tris. Within minutes he'd been put completely out of commission.

Love for him spilled from her heart to fill her whole body. He had an indomitable will, but like Samson who lost his great strength without his hair, Tris lay temporarily helpless from an old injury.

She climbed on the bed next to him. "Tris?" she whispered.

"Rachel—" He tried opening his eyes, but she could tell the natural light from the room caused him too much distress.

"Let me help you. Turn on your side away from me."

It took every bit of effort for him to do her bidding. The washcloth fell to the carpet, but it didn't matter. Once she had clear access, she placed hands around his neck and applied the special thumb massage to the back of his skull.

Her ministrations had stopped his migraine before. She hoped another miracle would take it away again. Within a few minutes she heard the change of tenor in his breathing. He was asleep.

She kept a constant vigil in case he needed something. Near the end of an hour, he changed positions and ended up turned toward her. Color had seeped back into his face. The carved lines around his mouth had vanished. No more shadows.

Rachel was finally able to relax. She rested on her side facing him. What a gorgeous man he was. It was a luxury to feast her eyes on him, but also a pleasure pain because she ached to trace his brows, the sculpted cut of his firm male jawline. His lips.

She'd done it many times before when they'd

lain awake on the cabin's bunk. He hadn't been suffering with migraine then. They'd studied each other's faces, so enraptured by the differences and so in love, the memories moved her to tears.

While she waited for signs that he was coming around, a drowsiness stole over her, slowly lowering her inhibitions. Her eyelids grew heavier. She fought sleep, but her emotions had been in such chaos, it was a losing battle.

"Oh, Tris…"

She could still see him through her lashes. But his brown eyes were open now. They didn't fight the light. Clear and free of pain, they looked into hers, finding a conduit all the way to her soul.

"Do you have any idea how beautiful you are?"

"As long as I'm beautiful to you, nothing else matters. I love you, Tris."

Instincts older than time drove her to seek that familiar place in his arms. She slid her hands around him to close any space left between them. Her lips sought his compelling mouth.

"Love me all night long like you did last night. Don't ever let me go."

"As if I would, *mon amour.*"

His mouth fastened hungrily over hers in an

explosion of deepest need. He pressed her down against the pillow. Their bodies and limbs entwined with such gratifying pleasure, they both moaned.

One kiss followed another. At first they took their time, pacing themselves to go slowly in order to relish the taste and feel of each other. But their insatiable craving started to get out of hand, creating a firestorm.

Tris infused her with a mounting ecstasy until she lived for nothing but his mouth. She couldn't contain her joy over being with him. Her emotions sought an outlet before they erupted.

"You're my life, Tris." She buried her face in his neck. "I don't ever want to get off the ship," came her feverish cry. "I couldn't live without you now."

"You won't have to. We're going to be together forever."

"That's what you promised, but you broke it. You broke it—" she sobbed.

"Rachel—wake up, *mon coeur.* You're having a bad dream."

She was dreaming?

The strong arms clutching her felt very real. She opened her eyes. The last thing she remembered was waiting for Tris to wake up.

To her amazement he was very much awake and molding the back of her head while he attempted to comfort her. His face was wet. So was hers. It came to her she'd been caught in the thrall of past euphoria with him.

"I—I was dreaming about us being on the ship," she stammered.

"I know. I was right there with you in living color. Once and for all I know how much you loved me and I loved you. We love each other now with even more intensity, so don't you dare deny it."

She started to tremble with excitement. "I won't."

He rocked her back and forth. "We're going to get married as soon as possible, just the way we planned. And then we're going to spend the rest of our lives making up for lost time by loving each other into oblivion. *Tu compris, mon amour?*"

"Yes, darling. I understand."

"Much as I'd like to pretend this bed is our old cabin bunk, and we have a whole week together before we have to come up for air, I don't dare stay here with you any longer. Papa would have my head if I got you pregnant again before we'd said our vows in church."

"I'm afraid my mother would be shocked, too."

Somehow she managed to disengage herself from his arms and slide off the bed. He steadied her so she wouldn't fall.

"Wooh—To be honest, I feel like I'm back on the ship."

He got to his feet and reached for her. "That was quite a journey we took. After what I experienced with you just now, I've stopped feeling cheated that you know something about our lovelife I don't. Well…maybe one or two details are still missing," he added in a wry tone.

Fire entered her cheeks, but she was no longer afraid to let him see the love that burned for him. When Tris was in a smiling, teasing mood like he was now, light illuminated her universe.

"I want to fill in that final memory for you. I've wanted it twelve years longer than you. You can't even imagine…"

"Rachel—" His dark head descended. Then he was crushing her mouth with his own. They clung to each other in their desperate need for assurance that this wasn't a dream.

"I was never complete without you," he whispered against her lips some time later.

"Neither of us was. In the children's own way, I think they both knew it."

Tris sucked in his breath. "We owe everything to Alain."

Her eyes moistened again. "I love him so much."

"He feels it. Speaking of the children, we need to tell them our news."

"You do the honors, darling. I know you're dying to."

His white smile dissolved her bones. He tucked a finger under her chin. "How is it you understand me so well?"

"At nineteen or ninety, certain things about you, Yves-Gerard Tristan de Monbrisson, will never change, thank heaven."

A solemn expression broke out on his handsome face. "I swear I'll never take our love for granted, Rachel."

"You think I don't know that?" She proceeded to kiss every arresting male feature. "Why do you imagine I fell in love with you in the first place?

"I may only have been eighteen, but when I looked into your eyes, I knew you were the *crème de la crème*. I'm never going to let you forget it," her voice trembled.

"Mom?"

"Uncle Tris? Is everything okay?"

"Let them wait," he said in a hushed, almost savage tone, pressing a hot kiss to her lips. "I don't want to leave this room yet. Hold on to me, Rachel. Pretend we're in that hurricane and all we have is each other."

"I don't need to pretend anything. Can't you see you've got me where I've always wanted to be? I'm not going anywhere."

e♦HARLEQUIN.com

The Ultimate Destination for Women's Fiction

Visit eHarlequin.com's Bookstore today
for today's most popular books at great prices.

- An extensive selection of romance books by top authors!

- Choose our convenient "bill me" option. No credit card required.

- New releases, Themed Collections and hard-to-find backlist.

- A sneak peek at upcoming books.

- Check out book excerpts, book summaries and Reader Recommendations from other members and post your own too.

- Find out what everybody's reading in Bestsellers.

- Save BIG with everyday discounts and exclusive online offers!

- Our Category Legend will help you select reading that's exactly right for you!

- Visit our Bargain Outlet often for huge savings and special offers!

- Sweepstakes offers. Enter for your chance to win special prizes, autographed books and more.

Your purchases are 100% guaranteed—so shop online at www.eHarlequin.com today!

eHARLEQUIN.com

The Ultimate Destination for Women's Fiction

For FREE online reading, visit
www.eHarlequin.com now and enjoy:

Online Reads
Read **Daily** and **Weekly** chapters from
our Internet-exclusive stories by your
favorite authors.

Interactive Novels
Cast your vote to help decide how these
stories unfold...then stay tuned!

Quick Reads
For shorter romantic reads, try our
collection of Poems, Toasts, & More!

Online Read Library
Miss one of our online reads?
Come here to catch up!

Reading Groups
Discuss, share and rave with other
community members!

For great reading online,
visit www.eHarlequin.com today!

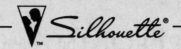

SILHOUETTE *Romance*

Escape to a place where a kiss is still a kiss...

Feel the breathless connection...

Fall in love as though it were
the very first time...

Experience the power of love!

Come to where favorite authors—such as

Diana Palmer, Stella Bagwell, Marie Ferrarella

and many more—deliver modern fairy tale
romances and genuine emotion,
time after time after time....

Silhouette Romance—
from today to forever.

Silhouette®
Live the possibilities